A Moment Lost

Elizabeth Butler

I was born in Kensington, London. I went to school in Hammersmith. I took English literature at St Marys University in London.

I worked at Heathrow airport as a customs officer for fifteen years, moved to Scotland and joined the Northwest writers group. I wrote plays for the local radio station. Married with two children, I have two dogs, 20 hens and numerous wild deer.

A Moment Lost

Elizabeth Butler

Matador
9 Priory Business Park,
Wistow Road, Kibworth Beauchamp,
Leicestershire. LE8 0RX
Tel: 0116 279 2299
Email: books@troubador.co.uk
Web: www.troubador.co.uk/matador
Twitter: @matadorbooks

ISBN 978 1788039 246

British Library Cataloguing in Publication Data.
A catalogue record for this book is available from the British Library.

Printed and bound in the UK by TJ International, Padstow, Cornwall
Typeset in 11pt Adobe Garamond Pro by Troubador Publishing Ltd, Leicester, UK

Matador is an imprint of Troubador Publishing Ltd

Proceeds are going towards Esther's charity in Ullapool

'How'd yer like them apples Grandad'

Esther 1992 -2013

1.

Eva Sinclair slowly opened her eyes and winced as she saw that her face was pressed painfully against the seat of a wooden bench. She put her hand up to her face and felt the ridges where the bench had cut into her cheek. Bewildered, she shook her head trying to understand what had happened. The whole of her body ached, probably, she thought, because of the uncomfortable position she had been lying in. How long she had been there she had no idea. Her head throbbed so violently that she had to lie still for a moment.

She attempted to swing her feet down on to the ground and sit up. As she did so, the contents of her stomach erupted. In an instant her clothes were covered with whatever she had consumed the night before. Gingerly she pulled herself into a sitting position, aware at the same time that her dress had ridden high above her hips, her underwear clearly visible.

Pulling her now sodden dress down, she looked shakily about. Although it was dark, slivers of light were emerging through the darkness. She gazed around bewildered. Had she been in an accident and was perhaps suffering from amnesia? That would account for feeling so awful but not knowing why. She discounted that idea. Although she had no knowledge of how she came to be here in this park – she knew it had to be a park by the openness of the surroundings – she was quite aware who she was. She groaned; her body ached but she didn't appear to have any injuries, so no accident.

She looked around again staring into the gloom, trying to identify some – any – familiar landmark. She felt almost lightheaded with relief when she thought she recognised where she was. Yes! She was sure the bench that she was sitting on was in a park she knew well, with tennis courts and a field where youngsters kicked a football around at the weekends. The scent of flowers was strong now as she gradually became aware of her surroundings.

Through the gathering light, she could make out the walled garden where the rose enclosure was. It was a place in which she and Brian liked to spend time whenever they could, grabbing a moment between their work, both enjoying listening to the children having fun on the swings and in the sand pit further along in the park. Aware of the state she was in now, she wondered whether she would ever look on this park in the same fond way again.

She could hear the birds now as they searched for food. It was a popular park, not too far from the centre of town. She had often seen young mothers here, and had wondered, at the time, when parents had stopped using prams for their babies. You rarely saw a pram now, so popular when she was young. She remembered how she loved to push her younger sister Sal around in the big white and black Silver Cross pram handed down from their grandparents. Now young parents used pushchairs, obviously finding them easier to manage.

Thinking now of those happy times she sighed wistfully; life seemed simpler in those days. She pulled her mind back to the situation now. She tried to still the racing of her heart; had she spent the night on this park bench? If that was the case, why? She had no memory of how she came to be here.

It was not yet daylight, but she knew that it soon would be. She looked anxiously about, aware of how she must look and worried now in case a passerby came along, or someone who knew her and saw her like this. She would be headline news: 'Judge found drunk on park bench'. She shivered, suddenly aware how cold she was.

Although it was still summer, the morning chill was eating through the thin dress she was wearing, now wet and clinging uncomfortably to her aching body. She knew she had to move... That was if she was able to; her head throbbed so much she felt faint with fatigue.

In the dimness of the early morning, she looked around the bench searching for her bag; it was nowhere to be seen. 'Just one more thing to add to this nightmare,' she muttered bitterly to herself. The bag was a favourite of hers. It had been a present from Brian. There hadn't been a lot of money in it. However, she would have to cancel her credit cards when she got home. Home! How was she going to do that?

A taxi was out of the question; not only did she have no money, but no self-respecting cabbie would allow her inside their cab looking – she grimaced – and smelling as she did now. She couldn't remember being or feeling so helpless. Since childhood, she seemed to know just where she was going and what she wanted from life; and apart from her parents split when she was a young girl, her life had gone the way she had more or less planned it.

Brian was away in Manchester attending a conference. She found her mobile which thankfully was still in her jacket pocket and very carefully removed it, grateful that it was still working, and dialled his number just to hear his voice and to convince her that this wasn't a dream. She wasn't surprised to get the unavailable tone. Brian would still be fast asleep.

Then she remembered that he had told her his phone would be turned off during the conference. Why hadn't she thought of that? God, what had she drunk last night? Last night! She had a sudden thought. David! Where was he? She sat still thinking about him, as the memory of the night before came back to her.

She had left the courthouse, where she worked as a district judge, after a day of listening to two young people who were divorcing, but not sure why they were doing so. She had told them to see a marriage counsellor to determine what was really going on in their lives. There was also a rather sad couple who were behind with their council tax. The last case to come before her was a couple squabbling over who should get custody of their dog after their divorce.

Any other time she might have been amused at their antics. However, it had been a long day, she was missing Brian, and wanted to get home, have a hot bath, maybe a glass or two of wine, and think about the decisions that she had made that day. She found it useful to do that. Sometimes, going over it later, she discovered she had made a bad judgement, and not as wise as it could have been. Thankfully this did not happen often.

Now, her head pounding fiercely, she forced herself to try to think clearly about the day before. She remembered that she had been thinking about the judgements she had made as she ran down the steps to her car.

4

She was one of the few members of staff who was afforded their own parking space. She was intent on looking for her car keys, so missed seeing David until he had caught hold of her arm.

'Whoa there, Eva, what's your hurry?' He was a tall man. She knew many women found him attractive, his fair hair carelessly falling across his brow. He wore the look that Eva had seen many times before. His normally good-natured grin carried a smugness she knew well. It was evident that he was going to impart news that she hadn't heard about.

'David, I didn't see you there,' she said gently pulling her arm free. 'What's up?' She and David had been close friends for some years now, and for a brief period they had been more than friends. It hadn't been serious stuff, from her point of view at least. Looking back at their relationship now, from an analytical point of view, she supposed that she had been using him to get her floundering life back on track. 'What are you up to?' she had asked again, aware that he was following her still grinning.

He was a councillor at the council offices and chairman of the planning department. He had an exuberant personality, forever seeing the amusing side of life, sometimes shocking Eva with his slant on even the most gruesome of things. She supposed it had been this that had first attracted him to her. It had jolted her out of a form of self-pity that had gripped her at that time.

She knew, however, that he took his job, and the decisions he and his committee made, seriously. His offices were a few doors away from the courtrooms where she worked. They often had lunch together, enjoying the close friendship they had managed to keep despite the fact that she knew that he still had deep feelings for her.

'Eva, who is the one person you would like to meet?' he had asked standing in front of her.

'Okay,' she had sighed, 'let's have it your way, David. The Pope, George Clooney, shall I go on?'

'Be serious, Eva,' he had laughed. 'What if I told you that I have an invitation to listen to a lecture given by Professor Alan Shaw tonight?' He had her attention now.

'You have been invited to hear Alan Shaw talk? How come?' She found this hard to believe. The great man was a legend, and very frail. It was rare for him to give lectures now. She remembered it being announced just recently that he had won the Nobel Prize for Literature. How had David managed to get hold of an invite?

'Yes, I was surprised too,' he said seemingly reading her mind. 'A gone friend from work gave it to me... must think he owed me a favour.'

'Nice for you, David,' she told him, trying hard not to sound peevish. She had tried to get to see the professor last time he had come to the town for a visit, quite a few years ago. But she had been unlucky due to the amount of people applying to hear one of his lectures. Now here was David telling her that he had somehow got hold of an invite. 'Jealousy will get you nowhere,' she had muttered to herself.

'Like to come?' he had asked, laughing at her expression, clearly enjoying himself.

'Really?!' She had been taken aback, surprised that he was asking her to go with him. She knew that he still loved her, but he was very popular and there was no shortage of people, especially women, he could have asked. She had hesitated; she would have given a lot to see the famous author, and she felt that she had been working hard lately and deserved a break. Aware that she was going to accept David's invitation, she felt a guilty pang: Brian would have liked to have heard the professor's talk too, but he wouldn't be back until tomorrow. 'Thanks, David.' She tried hard not to sound surprised. 'I would love to come. I will have to go home and change first though. Could you pick me up?' She was tired, but this was an opportunity that didn't come along that often. Suddenly the fatigue she had been feeling all day disappeared. Thanking him she waved goodbye as she climbed into her car and drove home, excited to be going to see the one person she admired so much.

When she had been a student studying law, the professor had visited her university as a guest speaker. He spoke about the way laws can be interpreted. In some countries, especially ones that he had visited, he had been shocked to discover that democracy was unknown in so many. They seemed to make up their own laws. He told the listening students to fight for what they felt was right. His fervour had made a deep impression, making her study more, determined to do well. She had followed his career with interest. To get a chance to hear him speak again was something she couldn't turn down.

David had agreed to pick her up outside her place later on, to give her time to change into more suitable clothes. The sombre grey suit she had worn in chambers lay discarded as she had a quick shower and changed into a light blue shot silk dress with jacket. It was still warm for this time of year, and she knew that the colour suited her. It was one of the extravagant buys she had treated herself to when she and Brian had decided to move in together.

She had just time to phone Brian, leaving a message on the hotel's answering machine, where he was attending a conference. He was hoping that the people who would be at the conference would be sympathetic to what he and his committee were involved in. He knew that what was planned would be a big asset to the whole community. He told her that he hoped the investors that were going to be there would also see the good prospects in it. The fact that the council was taking its time endorsing their plans was holding them back, but Brian was positive that his figures would convince the doubters that it would be a good investment.

Dave had picked Eva up outside her flat, commenting on how great she looked. She was excited, eager now to hear the lecture. She had never forgotten the professor's speech, although it had been years ago. She knew that it was through his example that her career had moved in the direction that it had. She had even wondered whether she might get a chance to meet him so that she could tell him how he had changed her life.

It hadn't taken long to arrive at the Cavendish Rooms where the great man was speaking. As in most towns, there is a lull between workers travelling home in busy traffic and when they emerge again for an evening's relaxation, so the drive to the rooms where the professor was speaking was without incident, the roads mostly clear of traffic.

It was a large building which looked austere in the daylight, but lit up as it was when they arrived, it gave Eva the impression of quiet grandeur. She had been to these rooms before for conferences and meetings; she had even given a speech there once. But that had been business; tonight would be fun. She would be able to tell Brian all about it.

Once inside Eva looked around. Unlike the times she had attended meetings there, where a long table in the centre of the room surrounded by hard chairs was a sign to those attending that business was the order of the day, now comfortable chairs were grouped together around a small platform. Soft lighting on the walls and drinks served by a waiter as people made their way to their seats gave the impression that an enjoyable evening was indicated.

Soft music added to the relaxed atmosphere. Eva had gratefully accepted the glass of wine the waiter offered her as she settled back in her chair. David had ordered a large glass of orange juice. When she looked surprised he had grinned.

'I have to have my wits about me tomorrow, Eva. The council are discussing a couple of big planning applications. I need to be clear-headed. I think that it will be tough going, but I intend to get my point across come what may.'

Eva couldn't question him further as the lecture was about to begin. However, she did wonder whether Brian's application was on the agenda. He had been waiting a long time for it. He was hoping that he would get the okay for the plans he and his board had submitted. They settled themselves in the comfortable chairs – they had decided earlier that they would grab something to eat afterwards. It would still be quite early and not having eaten anything beforehand, Eva was looking forward to rounding off the evening with dinner. Sipping her drink, Eva noticed David only took a tentative sip from his. She had wondered if he was worried about the agenda the next day. He had never discussed with her any of the plans that the council needed to approve, including the centre, which Brian and his committee had drawn up, and she had never asked.

9

She had been surprised that so few people were seated around to listen to the professor's talk. She had thought that there would have been many more. He was such an important figure in the world of travel as well as literature. David had explained, however, that because of the age of the professor, only a few select people were invited. Again Eva had wondered who the friend was who had left the council offices and had thought so much of David that they had given this invitation to him. The professor was introduced, and Eva understood the need for such a small audience as she watched, amid the applause, a stooped elderly man being helped onto the small stage which had been erected for him to speak from. The microphone had to be adjusted, which was carried out by his aide. Eva had doubted at the time whether the people who had come to hear him talk, although small in number, would have heard what was being said without the aid of the microphone, he spoke so softly.

He had aged since Eva had last seen him; nevertheless she listened enthralled as he outlined his career and how he came to write his book which had won such literary acclaim. He explained that it was about the travelling which had taking him all over the world, and although he was grateful for the award, he told them that he had more to do, and more of the world to see.

He had looked very frail and after a while, he seemed to have trouble speaking. Apologising, he made a signal to his aide, and a large man helped him off the platform. He left the room amid applause from an appreciative but concerned audience. Eva remembered that David had taken her arm and followed the rest of the people as they filed out into the warm night air. That was the last clear memory she had. She remembered nothing more until she had woken up on the park bench.

Sitting on that bench now, not able to describe the utter revulsion she felt as she looked down at her now ruined dress, and holding back the nausea she still felt, Eva rang David's number. She wondered where he had got to. Perhaps she had staggered to this park on her own, and he had lost sight of her after the meeting, when he had left her to get his car. He might be still around looking for her, and could pick her up, but as with her call to Brian, it went unanswered. She dialled the only other person that she could trust.

'I will cut your balls off if it's you, Nigel,' a sleepy bad-tempered voice said. Eva was so glad to hear her friend's voice.

Her own voice shook when she spoke. 'It's me, Nikki. I can't explain now, but I have a bit of a problem. Do you think that you could pick me up? I don't have my car. If you are able to, that is.'

Even in the state she was in Eva smiled grimly; she would have a real problem if Nikki had refused her request. She continued, 'I'll be outside Elms Park main entrance, and please, love, hurry.' All this said in a rush, and to her friend's ears, Eva's last words had held a note of panic. Her friend knew Eva well; this had to be serious stuff.

It was getting lighter; Eva knew that it wouldn't be long before people began to go about their business. She couldn't be seen looking like this. In spite of the doubt she had briefly felt, she was confident that her friend knew her well enough to figure out that her request was out of the ordinary.

'I'm on my way,' was all her friend said.

Although Eva was desperate, she also felt guilty: Nikki was going through a difficult time at the moment, she certainly didn't need this added complication. Feeling dizzy with fatigue and disgust with herself, Eva walked unsteadily towards the park's entrance, looking around for any sign of the park attendant, or an early riser walking their dog. Luckily early morning traffic had not yet started in earnest, but she was alarmed to see people walking past the park; she was sheltered from view, however, by the large columns which housed the entrance. Eva hoped that the early risers would not notice her.

2.

Eventually Nikki's yellow Mini drew up. Her friend gave a quick glance at Eva's clothes, and quickly wrapped a blanket around her. She didn't say a word, although Eva was aware of her friend's raised eyebrows as she opened the car door so that Eva could sit in the passenger seat. She asked Nikki if she could go to her friend's house first to clean up. Her own neighbour was lonely and inclined to watch what was going on; she didn't want to have to answer awkward questions her neighbour might ask.

To Eva's mind, that journey to Nikki's place had to be one of the worst that she could remember. Her filthy dress was sticking to her, she still felt ill, and her mind was in chaos wondering what had happened the night before. Where had David got to? She wished that she could remember. She was frustrated at how helpless she felt. It had been an uphill struggle to get where she had got to in her career. It had involved a lot of hard decisions and toughness on her part. She wasn't used to this feeling that events were out of her control.

Later, sitting in Nikki's kitchen, a cup of coffee in her hand and feeling human again after a shower and wearing her friend's clothes, Eva watched as Nikki's two children ate their breakfast. Beth, the older of the two girls, curiosity alive in her eyes, started to question Eva. She was saved from answering her by the girl's mother.

'Daddy's taking you to school this morning, girls, so hurry and finish your breakfast.' Eva was fond of Nikki's daughters and normally would have delighted in talking to them. Now, however, she was grateful for her friend's intervention. She wanted desperately to get home and try to figure out what had happened the night before. She would phone David to find out where he had got to, that is, after giving him a piece of her mind.

Her friend carried on talking small talk as she got the two girls ready for school. Eva caught a glimpse of Nigel as he opened the car door for his daughters to get in. He gave a quick glance and a wave to his wife as he drove away. Eva had always found him a quiet man, and the very opposite to her friend, who was outspoken and some would say loud, but Eva was fond of her, having known her since they had been at university together, and she valued her friendship.

Nikki and Nigel had agreed to separate for a few months to give them both a chance to review their marriage. Her husband, although agreeing with Nikki to split up for a while, had told Eva that he had no idea what was going on in his wife's mind. She had told him she needed more time, and he had accepted that. Eva liked Nigel and felt sorry for their problems, but realised it was none of her business; she knew only too well what could go wrong in a marriage.

She had married when very young herself. She had met Stephen, an up-and-coming architect, when she had been studying law, and for two years she had lived in a wonderful dream. She fell pregnant a year after they were married, and gave up her studies to stay at home. She lost the baby, and the dream ended.

After the miscarriage, she was told that she would be unable to have any more children. Eva was desolate, needing Stephen more than ever. But he became distant and started staying out late. Eventually he had told her that he couldn't stay in a marriage with no hope of having a family. He filed for divorce, which she didn't contest. At the time she had felt bitter towards him, and even more so when later she had heard that he had remarried and now was the father of twins. Luckily he and his new wife had moved away. She didn't think that she could have borne seeing Stephen's wife and children living near to her, knowing that this might have been her life had things been different.

As it was she had returned to college, gained a law degree, and had buried herself and her pain in hard work, which paid off as she took the bar exam and passed. She had shared offices with twelve other barristers. When eventually she was appointed district judge, it had helped to stave off the overwhelming loss she had felt, but it had taken a long time.

The bitterness she had felt at that time had got her through the many nights of loneliness, until slowly she realised that the hurt had eased, thanks to the new life that she had carved out for herself and the support of her family, although she still mourned her dead baby. They had told her at the time that it had been a boy and in her heart she had named him Billy. She sometimes talked to him. She knew that it was foolish, but it had comforted her in her dark moments. She smiled to herself. How she loved her life now, albeit different to how she had thought it would be; now she had Brian.

She had met him at a fundraising event, which her friend Beattie had coaxed her into going to. He was director of the charity that had organised the evening. They hoped to raise awareness as well as helping to raise money for the big project in the town. He and his committee had proposed a centre, built in the hub of the town, incorporating in it a drugs centre where advice and therapy could be found, as well as giving advice on the law, and matters relating to it.

Brian had been the main speaker there. He made a tall, gangling figure as he stood looking nervously about. He explained, his voice deep and rich, that this was the first time he had addressed the public in this way and was a little nervous. He needn't have worried; the people there had warmed to his openness and candour.

Eva had also been impressed by his sincerity, convincing her as well as others that what they had in mind would benefit the whole community. Afterwards Beattie had introduced them. He had thanked Eva for the donation she had given. He had taken her hand and asked for her phone number, with the intention, he said, of informing her how the money raised had been spent.

She found that she was attracted to him, but nervous too; her last involvement with a man had been David Sharpe, which had been some years ago. Since then she had found most of her time was caught up with court business, though she had confessed to Nikki that her work was really an excuse. She realised the truth was that she was a little afraid of hurting anyone else as she knew she had hurt David.

She thought it quite ironic that she herself had been terribly hurt by her first husband, and then she had hurt David – perhaps life is about hurting and getting hurt. *Does it make a person stronger?* she wondered. She had been hurt by Stephen's desertion, but had it made her stronger? She didn't know the answer to that. The experience had certainly changed her. She sometimes thought that she was incapable of loving again after Stephen had let her down so badly.

Two days after the fundraiser, Brian had phoned her and asked her out for a meal. Surprised but delighted she had accepted. Later she wondered why she had done that. There had been plenty of opportunities in the past, but she had always declined their invitations saying that she was not ready for any complications in her life. But she was glad that she had accepted this time. She had liked him from the start… his smile as he spoke was attractive. She remembered how he had told the people at the fundraiser what he and his committee hoped to achieve, his eyes washing over everyone there, pulling them into his way of thinking.

He had taken her to a little restaurant which served mostly Italian food. Eva had found herself eating dishes she rarely ate, aware how fattening some of them were. She had thought, as she watched him talking excitedly about the dream he had of improving people's lives once the centre was up and running, how different from Stephen he was, who had seldom got excited over anything he was involved in. She had chided herself then for comparing the two men. She realised that she wasn't fair to either; they both had they own, if different, qualities.

Although excited at being asked out by Brian, Eva was also wary. She gradually relaxed, enjoying the feeling again of being thought special by – she grinned to herself – a rather cool man. She found too that they had a lot in common. He seemed to know a lot about the law; she supposed being a director of a charity, it was natural that he should have some knowledge of it. They laughed at the same things. It was a long time since she had really enjoyed herself with the opposite sex; David was fun, but she regarded him almost as family. She was a little regretful when the evening was over; she had felt so comfortable when she was with him. When they reached her flat, she had horrified herself by inviting him in for a coffee, and then flushed in embarrassment when he had declined, telling her that he had an early business meeting the following morning. Sitting in front of the mirror later, she groaned at what she had done. What had made her do that? Thinking to herself that that was the end of that, she was certain that she would not hear from him again.

But she did. He had phoned her the following day inviting her out again. They saw each other regularly after that, both enjoying being together. He never referred to that evening until sometime later, laughing ruefully at the memory; Eva had asked him the reason why he hadn't taken her up on her invitation. He had shaken his head, telling her as he stroked her hair, 'It was too soon, I didn't want to spoil things, and I knew that I would be seeing you again.'

And they had, going to places that she as a single woman had found uncomfortable going to on her own. He had taken her to a well-known gambling club in London's heartland. She had lost £20 and complained laughingly all the way home convinced that the tables were loaded. Her heart beating, Eva knew that things were beginning to get serious between them.

One afternoon, he had picked her up at the courthouse telling her that he was taking her to see his baby. This turned out to be a large empty space, very grubby, with mud which clung to her shoes. She saw that it was mainly scrubland, very uneven with potholes everywhere, but Brian seemed excited over it, unlike herself, who merely saw it as a place the public used for tipping their unwanted rubbish.

He started explaining, however, as they walked around, how the centre that was planned to be built there would look. As he talked, she began to see it in a different light – from his point of view – and it took shape in her mind, sounding as though it would be an attractive focus for the town, and certainly better than it was now.

As they had got back into the car, he had produced a ring, grinning wryly and saying that had the car been bigger, he would have knelt before her. He asked her to marry him. His proposal didn't come as a complete surprise to her. She had known he would do so, but she was not looking forward to it when he did… She wasn't looking forward either to trying to explain to him in a way that she hoped he understood why she was turning him down. He knew about her failed marriage. She was certain that she loved him but… she had hesitated, not wanting to tell him that she did not trust him; her experiences with Stephen had clouded her opinion of marriage. She was sure that she did… all the same…

Brian had looked hurt and surprised. It occurred to her that he had never considered the possibility that she might say no to his proposal of marriage. She didn't think that it was his ego which made him so sure of her; she guessed he had thought it a natural progression. Shocked at her answer, he had asked her why she wanted to wait when they loved one another. She had no explanation to offer. However, she had stood her ground not really knowing why, and he had reluctantly agreed to wait.

It was at his suggestion that they moved in together. Eva knew that she couldn't bear to give up her flat. It had been the one move which had paved the way for her recovery after her marriage had ended. It had taken all her savings and promises to the bank to repay the money borrowed from them, and she had done it.

Brian had moved into her spacious flat. She was not sure how she felt when he had brought some of his furniture with him and moved hers to make room for them. It didn't look like her home anymore, but eventually she realised that it was both their home now. Loving him as she did, she had found herself waiting for him to arrive back, longing for his arms around her. He told her that she would see how much he loved her, and change her mind.

She was not used to sharing her inner thoughts. Stephen had not encouraged confidences. He had seemed to want her to be above the need for assurances. This she had done. Brian was different in so many ways. He listened whenever she wanted to talk. She found herself sharing secrets she hadn't even told Stephen. She felt guilty asking Brian to wait when she knew that they were good for each other, and often felt she was not being fair to him.

3.

She dragged her mind back to her problem now. As she told a wide-eyed Nikki what had happened the previous evening, her friend shook her head in disbelief.

'Come on, Eva, just how much did you drink? You must have had a loadful, and you haven't mentioned lover boy. Why did he leave you?' Nikki was puzzled; although she didn't know David she had seen the condition her friend had been in. Eva was always in control of herself; in Nikki's opinion too much so. This was unlike her.

Thinking about it now, Nikki found it hard to believe that her friend had been the worse for wear because she had drunk too much. It was Eva who often had to remind Nikki that she ought to ease up. She was usually so careful how her actions might be interpreted. As fond as she was of her friend, Nikki had always felt she should relax more. She grinned to herself; well, she certainly had now.

'Oh, Dave's not so bad,' Eva told her, 'but ever since I woke up on that bloody bench I wondered where he had got to. In fact I don't know why I am defending him, and if he were to walk in that door at this moment, I would give him a rollicking.'

Sitting beside her friend as Nikki drove her home, Eva was thinking of David and what had happened after the

21

lecture. He had not acted any differently to how he normally did. She remembered that he had taken her arm, telling her that he would bring the car over. He had parked just across the road to the Cavendish Rooms. She hadn't seen him cross the road – probably unconscious herself by then. David was gregarious and liked to shock people, but she had never known him to behave in such a way, leaving her when she clearly had not been coherent. He must have seen the way she was; it didn't make any sense.

He had a responsible job as executive head of the planning committee in the council chambers near to where the courthouse stood. The other councillors seemed to hold him in high regard, listening intently to what he had to say if he had a different point of view from the rest. But though sympathetic, they would go their own way in the voting.

She knew that David was fair and good at what he did, although many of the other councillors were older than he, and some clearly had resented the fact that he had done so well, but the work they did seemed to go quite smoothly despite this. Eva found him amusing, but often had to take him to task at some of the inflammatory stories he told her, and over the years that she had known him, she had got used to the outrageous comments he sometimes came out with, but they were usually harmless. In spite of this, she had never known him to deliberately hurt a person's feelings or leave a friend high and dry as he had done to her.

Nikki drew up at Eva's flat. 'Now, kiddo, keep in touch, let me know what that worm has to say for himself.' Giving Eva a hug she drove off in her sporty bright yellow Mini. Eva watched her friend, a frown on her face. In spite of her own troubles, Eva knew that her friend was worried about where her and Nigel's life was going. Nikki was very impulsive, and although Eva didn't know the entire story, she thought it a bit premature to be seeing a lawyer, which Nikki had said that she was considering doing.

The flat she and Brian shared was one she had purchased some years ago. Eva was proud of the fact that she had done it alone. She knew of course that her parents would have helped, but she was determined, and through sheer hard work she had managed it. She liked the way the house was close to her work. She looked at the flat now, enjoying the fact, not for the first time, that it belonged to her, her bit of independence. It was a red-brick building, with attractive gables at each end. Because it was a ground floor flat, they were fortunate to have a small garden, just big enough to house a tiny shed, where the lawn mower was kept.

She found the spare key Brian and she had hidden away in case of situations such as this. She was aware that her elderly neighbour was looking at her from her window above. Eva was thankful that she had had the forethought to go to Nikki's house first. She felt the urge to wave and did so. Her neighbour's face disappeared from her window.

Eva smiled to herself as she let herself in. Change her clothes, she thought, then tackle David. First off though, she cancelled her credit cards and inquired whether any had been used since the following day. She was assured that none had. She wondered what sort of person would steal from someone whilst they were so helpless looking. She moved towards her bedroom, intending to change into something else as the doorbell rang. Her first thought was that it was David himself coming to eat humble pie. She opened the door and saw two men standing there.

She recognised the taller of the two. Detective Inspector Peter Marsh was a very career-minded police officer with whom she had often come into contact in the courtroom. She smiled to herself as she remembered that he had asked her out several times in the past but she had declined; it seemed a bad idea to date anyone so closely involved with her work. However, that was before she had met Brian. She had a lot of time for Peter; he was both diligent and smart. With him was another, younger, detective, whom she didn't know too well. She was used to seeing the policeman during her working hours, when he was giving evidence against someone who had been arrested, but rarely, if ever, outside of the working environment.

'What is it?' She suddenly felt alarmed. Had something happened to Brian, or her parents? Silently she ushered them into her large comfortable kitchen. 'What's happened?' she asked unconsciously holding her breath. 'It's about Councillor David Sharpe,' Peter Marsh told her, not giving her a chance to wonder any longer. 'He was hit by a car last night, which didn't stop. I am afraid he died before he reached the hospital.'

Stunned, Eva put her hand to her mouth in horror. She swayed and clutched at the table to steady herself. Shock of finding herself on the park bench in the awful state that she had been in, and now hearing about David, was too much for her. Both men jumped forward to help her, afraid that she was going to faint. She pulled herself together, annoyed with herself for showing a moment of weakness. She stared at the two men.

'That's not possible, I was with him last night... I'm alright,' she told them waving them away as she turned shocked eyes towards the two detectives. 'We went to hear a lecture together.' She found it hard to believe that David, so alive and exuberant, should have been killed, perhaps at the same time she had become unwell. It was not like him to be that careless on the road. 'He said that he was going to bring the car across.' She didn't add that was as much as she remembered.

'Yes. We know that.' Marsh opened his notebook. 'We have a witness, who recognised you at the lecture. Did you see anything? The car maybe which knocked him down after the lecture? Is there anything that might help us in our investigations to find out what happened? For instance, do you remember how you got home? It obviously wasn't with Mr Sharpe.'

'I am afraid that I can't remember a single thing after the lecture was finished,' she told them flushing. She hated to be in this position. She was used to taking charge of a situation, aware too that she had avoided answering his question.

'Yes, our witness did say that you seemed the worse for wear. You must have had quite a lot to drink by what this witness has told us.'

'Who is this witness that saw me, and knows so much about the state I was in?' Eva was annoyed.

'You know that I can't reveal the names of witnesses,' the inspector said stiffly.

She did know that, but she felt frustrated to think that someone she knew, or at least knew her, saw her like that. *Help!* she thought; it could be any one of the dozens of people she came into contact with during her court sessions. Her heart stopped; it might even be her immediate boss Judge Hawkins. She smiled grimly; that was all she needed.

She knew he had no time for women in the Judiciary and would be delighted to hear about her exploits.

She tried to remember what had happened before everything went hazy. There were probably people at the lecture that were well known. A lecture given by anyone as famous as Professor Shaw was bound to bring them out, but she hadn't known any of them personally when she had looked around her, which gave her some comfort; she would certainly have recognised the judge if he had been there.

Perhaps this phantom onlooker saw that she had in fact had only two glasses of wine. He or she seemed to know everything else that she did. She felt unusually angry. She was in the dark about her movements afterwards. Now hearing that David had been knocked down made her feel even more helpless. Where had she been at that time?

Why had it happened? Even her best friend chose to think that it was just a blip on her part, that she had just drunk too much. She felt the need to defend herself.

'Inspector Marsh,' she said addressing him in the same tone that he had used, 'I can assure you that I did not have too much to drink. I must have been ill. The lecture with Professor Alan Shaw lasted under an hour. The poor man was taken ill before he had finished speaking. How much can one drink in such a short a time?' She realised, however, that what she was telling him was hard to believe even to her own ears. She remembered her own youth and the incredible amount of alcohol she could knock back as a student. She thought back, searching her memory, trying to recall the two glasses of wine the waiter had given her. Had she had more than that? Surely she would have remembered. 'What matters, Judge Sinclair,' his voice still formal, 'is that you were not involved in the accident as far as you know. You say you did not see Mr Sharpe cross the road or the car that hit him, and you can't remember how you got home. We shall have to see what we can find out regarding that. You obviously can't help us any further with our investigations. If anything does come back to you, well, you have my number.' He turned at the door. 'Is there anything else that I need to know?' he asked.

Feeling numb with all that had happened, and at what the inspector had told her about David, she watched in silence as he and his partner walked across the room to the door. With a start she remembered her handbag. Perhaps they might find out what happened to it, not that she expected it to turn up. She wouldn't mention the fact that it could still be in the park. She told Marsh that she had lost it. He made a note of the description, and took his leave.

'I will get back to you on that,' he told her, adding, 'I am sorry about Councillor Sharpe, Eva, I know he was a friend of yours.'

She thanked him and watched as both men got into their car and drove away. She knew that she should have mentioned the fact that she had woken up on a park bench, but shame and the feeling that as a judge her behaviour outside the courtroom ought to be above reproach had kept her from saying anything to the inspector.

She sighed as she went back into the kitchen trying to work out what could have happened. When had she become separated from David? Where was she when he had been knocked down? How had she got to the park? Had she walked there herself? The witness had told the police that she looked completely out of it. If that was the case, how had she done that? She knew that Elms Park was only a few yards away from where the lecture had taken place, but still she did not believe that she had gone there under her own steam. Who was this witness? She felt drained with all the questions drumming around in her head.

Although it was still early afternoon, and she still hadn't changed out of the clothes given to her by her friend, she felt that she needed to sit down and think. Her grief at hearing about David had left her drained; there was too much to take in. She poured a drink for herself. Settling into the big chair that was in the kitchen – a comfortable one that both she and Brian claimed – she mused sleepily that she must ring Nikki as her eyes closed, and before long, she was fast asleep.

She dreamt that strong arms were around her. She smiled, feeling safe for the first time since she had woken up in the park. She opened her eyes and saw Brian smiling down at her. She jumped up guiltily and threw her arms around him. She noticed as she did so how dark it was outside. She must have slept for hours.

'Hey,' he laughed, 'I'll have to go away more often.' He saw the empty glass on the table. 'Got one for me? I could use one.'

Eva saw now that he had a frown on his face. It was unlike him to bring his problems home. She did know, however, that the funding was going slower than he would have liked. He seldom confided in her. She supposed that being Brian, he was aware of her own responsibilities and tried to guard her against other problems.

'How did the meeting go?' She noticed the frown deepen on his face. 'Not so well, love?'

Her problems would have to wait. She poured him a

28

drink and watched with some concern as he knocked the glass back and drained its contents; she had never known him to drink like that. She smiled grimly to herself; they were both doing things that they never used to do. She watched as he eased himself into the chair with a sigh, the same chair that she had spent the day sleeping in. The rule of the house was: first one to get it, it was theirs.

'I needed that,' he said grinning sheepishly, handing the glass back to her. 'How have you been? I got your message. Was it a good evening?'

Eva smiled fondly at him; it was like him to think of her. She kissed him. She was reluctant to tell him all that had happened. She couldn't quite believe herself the events that had occurred while he had been away. She remembered how she had felt when she had opened her eyes and found herself on the park bench, the filthy dress clinging to her; the way her stomach had erupted. She was seldom physically sick, and she wondered why it had happened then.

'Never mind about me,' she told him brushing away her thoughts. 'I will fill you in later. First tell me what happened. You didn't get the promise of the funding that you were expecting?'

She knew that he had overspent on the project, he had told her that much. The consultants' and surveyor's fees were steep. Brian was relying on the grants and loans as costs had escalated. He had hoped to be able to tell his board that the promise of funding had been approved, so that the work on the centre could go ahead as soon as planning permission had gone through.

The people there, you know, the bloody bankers and

investors, refused to give any assurances of loans or funding, at least for the time being. They made it clear that unless we get approval for the planning application, they won't gamble their shareholders' money. I will, however, talk to them again as soon as the council stops dragging its heels.' His voice was bitter as he went on, 'What infuriates me is that this centre will benefit the whole town.' He rubbed his hand through his hair, his voice sharp with frustration, as he pulled her onto his knee hugging her.

'Oh, Eva, we live in strange times where the god is money and power.' He tilted her face and looked into her eyes.

'Let's forget about that. Tell me, did you miss me?'

'You will never know how much,' she told him fervently, knowing that events would not have happened the way they had if he had been there.

'Brian…' she began, but what could she tell him? That she had drunk too much and could be a witness to David's accident, but was she? She wished that she could remember. Surely she wasn't near him when the car hit him, but lying in the park, in a near-naked state. She shivered as she remembered her dress high up around her hips when she had woken up.

'What's wrong, love?' He looked searchingly at her. 'I've unloaded my troubles, now it's your turn. I can see that something is worrying you.' She knew that Brian was a good listener and she needed someone she could talk to at this moment. She related everything that had happened that evening, finishing with waking up on the park bench.

'I just can't remember anything after we had heard the professor speak. What an amazing man he is, Brian, he looked so frail yet he found time to tell us about where he was going after finishing his book. He seemed to fall ill or became too weak to carry on during the lecture because it was cut short, but what we heard was wonderful.' Eva smiled, remembering that part of the evening and how enjoyable it was.

'Then what happened?' Brian prompted her, frowning.

'Then nothing – or at least nothing that I can remember. The last thing that I do remember is David opening the door for me as we were leaving. I seem to recall that the few people left in the hall there were still clapping the professor even though he had left the stage, and David telling me to wait while he went to fetch the car over. I was feeling dizzy, that's all. I don't seem to be able to remember a thing after that. It all went hazy.'

'For God's sake, Eva, how much did you drink?'

The exasperation in his voice angered her. She glared at him. 'I don't understand you people. Nikki said the same thing: that I had drunk too much. Do you think that I am not capable of knowing when I have had too much to drink? I am telling you, as I told her: we were in there for only an hour or under that, I had two glasses of wine… that was it.'

Her face flushed with anger, Eva stared at Brian. How could he think that, knowing the responsible job she had with her court work? Brian could see that Eva was on the edge. She couldn't take much more.

'If you say that you didn't drink a lot, then of course I believe you, love,' he said scratching his head. 'I was thinking though, if that's the case, is it possible that something was put in your drink? I mean what about David? Would he be capable of doing something like that? Where did he get to? It's all rather suspicious if you ask me.' He was contrite, putting his arms around her, with a puzzled look on his face.

Eva stared at Brian; all the anger she had felt left her as she took in what he was suggesting.

'David liked a joke, but the idea of him lacing my drink is laughable. He just wouldn't have done that.' Eva was aware that she was speaking about David in the past tense, but Brian had not noticed. He kissed her forehead and gave a grim smile as he got to his feet, obviously thinking that she had told him everything that had happened that evening.

'Well, let's sleep on it. I for one am ready for my bed, you must be too. We both seem to have had a tough time. Let's have a nightcap, then bed, what do you think?'

'I haven't told you the worst part.' She bit her lip.

'There's more?' he exclaimed. 'Dave was knocked down by a car last night,' she told him. 'I believe he was killed outright. The car didn't stop. I didn't see the accident. The police came to see me when I got home. They told me about it. I just cannot believe it.' The horror of it showed in her face. Brian put his arms around her.

'My God, Eva, that might have been you. How awful for you and as for poor David… I can't believe it.'

Brian, though not knowing David well, liked him. The regret showed on his face as he took her arm. 'Tell me the rest tomorrow, my love, I am too tired to take it all in now.'

As she got ready for bed, Eva realised that she hadn't phoned Nikki; she didn't know about David yet, so much had happened. She would phone her first thing. She thought about her work at the court tomorrow; she had to have a clear head, she knew, but she didn't know how she was going to get through the day. She was thankful that she had had

32

a day off. She knew that she would have been unable to concentrate after all that had happened.

The morning seemed to come too soon. She had spent the night tossing and turning and had dreams that she couldn't quite recall but knew, as she dragged herself out of bed and got ready for work, that there was a threatening note to them. Brian was already up and preparing breakfast.

She could smell the tantalising smell of coffee and quickly showered, with a reminder to return Nikki's clothes to her. She quickly phoned her, telling her about David and that she would be in touch, cutting off the questions that her friend fired at her. Nikki was obviously shocked to hear about David although she hadn't known him personally and, like Brian, told Eva that she also could have been dead if she had been with David. Glad that was done, she got dressed. She wore the navy suit with a white silk blouse which Brian liked. She had always thought it rather dull, but today it matched her mood. Brian gave her an appreciative smile.

'You look none the worse for your adventure, Eva.' She knew that he was trying to make her feel better; she had noticed that her eyes had dark smudges under them. She sipped the coffee that Brian had made, thinking how much she loved him.

It was going to be a tough day all round: not only did she have a full casework to get through, but by this time all her colleagues would have heard the terrible news. They would be expecting her to know the answers to what had actually happened, still under the impression that she had been with David when the accident had occurred. Eva knew that Beattie, her law clerk, would be sympathetic, even though she didn't know the full story. She would, however,

33

lighten her casework, giving her just the important cases to see. Beattie knew the judge's commitment to her work was one of her strengths.

4.

Detective Inspector Pete Marsh looked down at the file on his desk. Had he missed something? On the face of it, Councillor Sharpe's death seemed like an accident, albeit the driver had not stopped. In Marsh's experience that wasn't unusual. If the driver had been drinking, he or she may have panicked and left the scene of the accident because of that. He put down the file while he sipped his coffee.

He wasn't too keen on this investigation, and hadn't wanted it. With a hit and run, it usually fell to a sergeant at the station and DCs to oversee incidents such as this. However, due to a serious disturbance at a rally, Sergeant Roger Smyth, who normally would have taken charge of this case, had lost an eye from a stone thrown. The crowd demonstrating had become excited and a couple of youths had seized the opportunity to attack the police.

After a long convalescence, the sergeant had returned to police duties. He had, however, found it difficult to carry out the normal workload that a sergeant would be called on to do. It was agreed to allow him to carry on working in a lesser capacity until he retired. This left Marsh the job to wrap it all up in what seemed like an easy case of hit and run. What worried Marsh now was the statement from the eyewitness that the councillor seemed to stagger as he crossed the road. He frowned as he looked at the witness statement. Something was off-key here. Eva had said in her statement that David Sharpe had not been drinking alcohol. He had spent the evening nursing a soft drink. Had he been feeling unwell? That might explain why he had staggered. There was a CCTV camera near to where the accident had occurred; hopefully it might show what had happened the evening of the lecture. He would get Bob to check that. In the meantime, he needed to speak to the witness who saw the accident; it could be that he might have remembered something else.

Marsh knew from experience that it often happened that the horror of seeing someone knocked down by a car and killed can make the mind numb; later, however, other facts are remembered. Our memories, though a wonderful computer, sometimes work in a strange way, letting us down when we need them most. Marsh thought that it was worth talking to the witness again to see if he had anything else to tell him. The uniform branch had spoken to him at the scene of the accident, but Marsh found it helpful to speak to them first hand.

'If you're not too busy chatting up the women, Detective,' he called. He had seen Bob outside his office talking to one of the women officers. He signalled the young detective to come in. 'We need to get this case sewn up,' he said sharply.

'Kate, I mean Constable Evans,' the young detective's face was crimson, but he continued, 'Constable Evans was telling me something that might be of interest to us, when she was walking past the town hall the other day.'

'Oh yes, and what would that be?' Marsh was still reading

the file, half-listening, but now he raised his eyes to look at the detective. 'Sorry, Bob, what were you saying about the councillor?' Marsh laid the file aside and listened to what the young detective was saying. Sometimes the younger officers, though not as experienced as others, had a good grasp on human relationships.

I was saying that the constable witnessed a rather heated argument between Councillor Sharpe and the chief clerk outside the council offices a few days ago – on the steps of the building in fact. They both looked angry, according, that is, to Constable Evans.'

'I wonder what that could have been about,' Marsh mused. 'There may be nothing in it to connect it with what happened but it's worth having a chat with… What's the chief clerk's name?' he asked and waited for the young detective to look at his notes.

'John Turner, sir. I believe he has been clerk there for a while now, long before Councillor Sharpe's election to the ward.'

'Perhaps it's just a rattling of sabres,' Marsh smiled, 'the young buck making a stand against the old rule.' He put the files away, picked up his jacket and walked to the door.

'We need to speak to Mr Sullivan, the witness who saw the councillor stagger when he crossed the road that evening. Also I would like a word with John Turner about his row with David Sharpe, not that I expect much. If we interviewed people because they fell out with someone, we would have our work cut out. I don't think our Mr Turner drove over Sharpe because of a tiff, but he might let slip the reason behind the argument, which may have some bearing on the case. Thank the constable for me. Sorry if I chewed you out earlier, you'll get used to the way I work. Good work anyway.'

The council offices which also housed the benefit offices as well as planning, council tax etc., was a large imposing building, sharing the dubious honour with the county court of being the oldest, and some would say the ugliest, building in the town. The two buildings were adjacent to one another.

They were shown into an outer office, and before long a tall pale-faced man entered. He had a pronounced stoop and a worried frown on his face. Marsh suspected the stoop and the frown were both products of the job he did. He walked towards them, his hand outstretched, which Marsh took.

'Well, gentlemen, I suppose this visit of yours has something to do with Councillor Sharpe's death. Terrible! Terrible.'

He bowed his head in mournful acknowledgement of the situation. Marsh, who was used to the different ways the public had of showing emotion, decided the man's face seemed expressionless; it held no regret about the councillor's untimely death.

'I'm sure, sir, but I would like to ask you a few questions about your relationship with the late Mr Sharpe.' Marsh saw the man drew in a sharp breath; it looked to the inspector to be more impatience than worry.

'We were colleagues and had a working relationship.' He bowed his head again; obviously, Marsh thought, the clerk was a man who weighed up his words carefully before he spoke.

'Inspector, is this relevant to David's unfortunate accident?'

'Mr Turner,' Marsh smiled thinly at the clerk, 'I don't know yet what is relevant. I didn't know Councillor Sharpe. I have to rely on his acquaintances to tell me what he was like.'

'I am afraid I don't understand. David was knocked down by some maniac who didn't stop. What more is there to find out?' He added, 'I don't know what else I can tell you, Inspector. I do have an awful lot of extra work due to the councillor's unfortunate accident.' He rose and extended his hand, which went unheeded as Marsh remained seated.

'Just one more question, sir, if you wouldn't mind,' he said. 'I believe that you and Mr Sharpe had some disagreement a few days before the accident. Can you tell me what that was about?'

'Inspector,' the clerk's voice became guarded, 'I would like to help, however, what we discussed was official council business. I am sure that you understand confidentiality in your line of work.'

'I do, sir, but surely one wouldn't discuss council business on the steps of the council offices, as has been reported.' Marsh saw the man's face grow pale with anger.

'I didn't realise that the police listened to gossip,' Turner replied stiffly, colour returning to his face. 'I have nothing more to say to you at this time, Inspector,' he said holding the door open. Marsh had to leave it at that. He knew that he would get no more out of the clerk. Once outside, the young detective voiced his doubts about what had been achieved.

'On the face of it nothing,' the inspector told him, 'but it is amazing what people will say when they don't like the questions that are being asked. I have given him something to think about, that's enough for now. Let's have a bite of lunch and then I want a word with…' he opened his notebook, 'ah yes, Mr Val Sullivan. He witnessed the accident, or at least he heard it. That is if it was indeed an accident, I can't rule anything out at this stage,' he said rubbing his chin thoughtfully. 'Why does that name ring a bell?'

He turned to the young detective. 'Bob, I want you to do a couple of things for me. Check the CCTV camera at the scene of the accident. I noticed it when I checked where the councillor was standing when the car hit him.' He looked down at the name in his notebook. 'See if you can find out anything about our Mr Sullivan.' Marsh stopped. 'On second thoughts, I won't interview Mr Sullivan yet, I will wait until we know more about him. Take Constable Evans with you, she sounds as though she has her wits about her.'

'Thanks, sir.' Bob smiled at his boss as he followed him into the café where they usually ate. He was guiltily aware that he had a football match to play that afternoon. It was an important game, and one that he hoped would move him up the ladder where the next step would be to become a referee. The young detective found that a good kick-about on the football pitch relaxed him. He would see to the couple of jobs that the inspector had asked him to do after the match. He hoped that the game would be over before he was asked what he had found out about the witness checks he had to do.

Returning to the office, the inspector was informed that the superintendent wanted to see him straight away. Superintendent Jim Townsend was a large man. He and Marsh had come through the ranks together, but whereas

Marsh was diligent and rarely, if ever, brought a case against a suspect unless he was certain of his facts, the superintendent was of the opinion, 'You treat them as though they are all guilty, and you will find that they often are.' It seemed to work too, his rise past Marsh was due mainly to this. Marsh had no axe to grind because of it. He worked in a different way to his boss. However, any summons to see him was met with a bit of trepidation from himself and any other of the officers below his rank. His colleagues had given the superintendent the name 'Quick Nick' because of the way that he would do his utmost to get a conviction from a suspect without the full evidence being obtained. Marsh didn't encourage the nickname, and often wondered at the same time what they called him in private.

'Come in, Peter.' The superintendent's voice matched his girth, which filled the chair he was sitting in. His booming voice could sometimes be heard down the corridor, much to the dismay of a detective who was getting a balling out. Marsh sat down. He looked at Townsend, trying to gauge which way this meeting was going to go; he had his answer when his boss shook his head, his jowls moving from side to side.

'Peter, I haven't had the finished report on the hit and run case yet, what's holding it up? It's a simple enough case. It surely doesn't take a detective of your rank to waste so much time over a hit and run. I can't afford the time you are taking to wind it up.'

'Which hit and run were you referring to, sir?' Marsh hedged. He had hoped that he would have a few more days to investigate the death of David Sharpe; perhaps then he would have something concrete to tell his boss. 'Don't be obtuse, Pete.' Townsend's frown deepened. 'I've had the commissioner on my back. Wrap it up, the family want closure. Why hasn't the councillor's body been released yet?'

Marsh groaned inwardly. He knew that his superior might not accept the explanation that he had: that he was not happy with leaving it as it is. He felt that there was more to it than just a hit and run. David Sharpe was a youngish man in his forties, and according to his file, fit and healthy. One expected elderly people, who would be slower crossing a road, to be victims of a road accident, not a man as young as Councillor Sharpe.

'I need more time, sir. I am still waiting for the results of the contents of Councillor Sharpe's stomach, along with the blood test.'

'Why in God's name are you interested in what the man ate? He was run over. Am I missing something?' Marsh's boss said testily staring at him.

'Witnesses have told me that the councillor had been acting strangely, staggering...'

'Good God, Peter,' his boss interrupted him, 'I expected even you to surmise that he had been drinking.'

'That's the point, sir,' Marsh said shaking his head. He was used to his boss's bluntness, as long as he could convince him to give him more time.

'He was driving that evening, and refused any alcohol and opted for a soft drink. I would like to know what else he had.'

'Well,' his chief said, his voice more subdued, scratching his chin thoughtfully, 'I grant you that it is interesting. Do you know if he took drugs?' Marsh could almost see the other man's ears prick up, obviously hoping for a more interesting conclusion, which it would be if it was found that the councillor had been high on drugs.

'That's one of the theories we can't rule out.' The inspector shrugged, his mind already on the checks he still had to make.

'That's something which needs looking into, I agree,' the superintendent looked interested, 'but don't drag it out, and keep me informed.'

Marsh hurried out, thankful that the interview had gone better than he had thought. The first thing was to get some answers from the forensics. They hadn't got back to him yet, but that wasn't unusual. It would be interesting to know whether the councillor had been ill after the lecture. That would account for the reason he had staggered when he crossed the road. He hadn't seen Bob around. He wondered if he had learnt anything regarding the CCTV near to the Cavendish Rooms where the accident had happened; he also wondered if he had run a check on Sullivan. Marsh hoped Bob had got some answers for him.

5.

Eva Sinclair walked up the steps of the courthouse, aware that more people than usual were gathered on them, discussing David no doubt. It was a fine day with hardly any wind. The flags on the court building lay still. Although it was warm, she shivered; she couldn't believe that David was dead. His had been a larger-than-life personality and he was popular with the staff here. A regular visitor to the courthouse, he seemed to have a joke or a clever quip with everyone he met. The council offices were close to the courthouse, and he would often pass the time chatting to the clerks there when he wasn't involved in council business.

Eva knew that there was a serious side to him though. She had been aware lately that he wore a deep frown on his face, which worried her. She was used to his flippant exchanges with those around him. It was not like him to look the way he did. Although she could not fathom out what was bothering him, she knew him well enough to know that something was. She had even asked him just recently if everything at work was alright; for a moment, she felt that he was going to tell her, but then he had grinned at her, a hint of mischief in his eyes.

'Do you think that I would tell you all my secrets?' he had laughed, and the moment was gone.

On the other hand, he had often interrupted her treasured breaks from hearings. At first she had felt resentful at the intrusion. Listening to sometimes quite petty grievances was tiring; to just sit in her chambers for a little while, before she tackled more woes in the courtroom, was a luxury for her. David would breeze in, no apologies, and sit sprawled in one of her armchairs. Her frowns often turned to smiles at his antics.

Sadly she remembered the last time he had invaded her space. She had finished for the day after a particularly involved defamation case; her belief in mankind was at its lowest ebb. On these days she wondered whether she was in the wrong job, as her patience with the public and their squabbles was sometimes hard to take. However, this feeling didn't last long. On this particular day, David had burst in, grabbed her around her waist and whirled her off her feet, her handbag falling from her hand, its contents scattering over the floor. David had helped her retrieve what had fallen out, picking up the last of her things.

'I often wondered what women judges kept in their handbags, now I know,' he had said handing the bag to her with a grin.

Beattie, her law clerk, was passing the door; her frown sent them both into fits of laughter. Beattie was a doppelganger for Kathy Bates. She could wither you with one glance. She was, however, Eva's refuge against the world. As her law clerk, she advised the judge on aspects of the law, and her knowledge was second to none. Eva relied on her to keep her judgments within the framework of the judiciary. She guarded Eva's privacy religiously; she was also a good friend. Laughing with Eva, David's smile changed to a frown as he glanced out of the window. Eva couldn't see what he was looking at, but then he turned to face her.

'Eva, do you think it possible that someone you trusted could ever do the dirty on you and let you down?' he asked, his face serious.

Eva studied him for a moment and then said, carefully choosing her words, 'I believe that we all have the capacity for wrongdoing, some more than others. To whom are you referring, Dave?' She remembered now that he had grinned.

'Oh, I'll sort it out,' he said, adding, 'There are not many people I trust, Eva, but you are one of them.'

She had been touched, but had wondered at the time who he had meant. She would never know now. She sighed as she thought about David; she would miss him and his antics so much.

She saw that her mail was on her desk. She glanced through it. Her clerks dealt with most of it, except private letters; she would see to those later. She was intrigued, however, by a large envelope and opened it feeling curious because it had 'Photograph' in large print stamped across the top of it. She drew it out and stared in horror at the photograph in front of her. It was of herself lying sprawled on the park bench, legs wide apart. She saw also that most of her underwear was plainly in view. Anybody looking at it would be in no doubt what she looked like: someone very intoxicated. Eva felt sick. Who had sent it, and what was their reason for doing so? She reached for the phone and dialled the inspector's number, knowing that she should have done this earlier.

'Inspector Marsh speaking.' Marsh's low voice filled her with dismay. She was ashamed of what she had to tell him.

'Peter, it's Eva Sinclair.'

'How are things?' His tone was different, softer then the last time they had met. 'If you are ringing up about Councillor Sharpe, I'm afraid I can't tell you much.'

'No, it's not about David,' Eva spoke quickly, 'at least I don't think so. Peter, I didn't tell you everything about that evening. I wonder if we could meet somewhere. I really don't want to go to the station, perhaps my place? Will six be okay? Hopefully I will be finished by then.'

Marsh said that would meet her and Eva replaced the receiver. She knew that she had done the right thing. If this was a blackmail attempt, it was best to get it out in the open; she might have to put up with awkward questions that were likely to be asked. She shuddered when she thought of the person who had taken the photograph; how vulnerable she had looked lying there. It had clearly not been an attempted assault, but for what reason could it be, other than to blackmail her in some way? But why?

Brian wasn't at home when she got there. He never phoned her at work, he might be interrupting something important. In any case, Eva had her phone off most of the time. There was a message for her on their answering machine, however, telling her that he was caught up in a meeting, and would be late. She sighed; Brian was a good person to have around when advice was needed. She wished that he was there now. She was not looking forward to what she had to tell the inspector. The doorbell went, and Eva saw Peter Marsh outlined through the frosted glass of the door. She was thankful that his assistant was not with him.

'Come in, Peter,' she said ushering him into the study. She made coffee, and they sat in silence for a moment.

He wanted to give her time to tell him whatever it was, in her own way. He had no idea what it might be, but the expression on her face told him that it was important and not easy for her to tell him.

'I'm so sorry, Peter,' she began, 'I should have told you what happened after the lecture.'

She was unable to meet his eyes. Her life up till then had been an open book with no secrets. Now because of what had happened after the lecture, she had not been truthful with her parents about what had occurred, or the police.

'Go on,' he prompted, and with a faltering tone, Eva told him everything, or everything that she remembered. When she had finished, he frowned and shook his head in disbelief.

'Eva, I am investigating David Sharpe's accident. I don't expect a judge of all people to withhold information from the police. Why did you?' he asked looking down at the notes he was making.

His voice was angry. She could hardly blame him; she should have been helping the police in every way possible to get to the bottom of David's death. She felt the reprimand was deserved and flushed guiltily feeling like the wayward child that she had been years ago.

'I have no excuse, other than I was too ashamed to tell you. I am sorry.' She didn't have anything else to say. She sighed as she picked up the photograph and handed it to him.

'But now this. I received it earlier. Do you think that it's a blackmail attempt?'

Marsh drew in his breath as he looked at the photograph.

'You should have told me about that evening of the lecture and all that had occurred earlier. Do you realise that a man died that night? A man you were with. I expected more of you, Judge Sinclair.' Eva's face flamed as he continued, 'I will check this out. There was nothing else in the envelope? I will borrow this if I may.' As she nodded, he went on, 'Perhaps the lab may be able to find something that might help us.' He sipped his coffee. 'Is there anyone you think may have a grudge against you, perhaps someone you have come up against in the courts?' She stared, still stung by the inspector's earlier words.

'Peter, I listen to a driver who might argue that £60 is too dear a fine for a ten-minute wait, or a tenant who owes his landlord money. Can you see any of these people going to so much trouble because I didn't agree with them? No, it's got to be something else.' She sighed; she had never felt so helpless. She regarded herself as someone who could be strong in adversity. Where was that feeling now? He stared at her for a moment, still angry, and then he rose from his seat and patted her shoulder, understanding a little why she had acted as she had. She smiled up at him, grateful for that small action.

'Not a very official reprimand after my actions, Inspector.' She spoke light-heartedly; neither of them heard Brian enter the room until he spoke.

'What am I missing?' he asked, a deep frown on his face.

Eva ran to him laughing as she hugged him. 'Ninny, Peter was consoling me over something that I got in the post. I will tell you all about it later,' then turning to the inspector, 'Is there anything else you need to know? I am so sorry for not being open with you,' she told Marsh walking with him to the door.

'Not at the moment, Eva. I will need you to come down to the station sometime to make a statement. I will let you know if I find out anything of interest.'

He saw Brian watching them from the room. He said a quick goodbye, thinking to himself as he went towards his car that he hoped Brian knew just how lucky he was. She had made a mistake not informing the police straight away; it might have led to a swifter conclusion, one couldn't tell in cases like this. On the other hand, he had always admired her ability to look dispassionately on a case she was listening to in her courtroom while giving it a fair ruling.

'I have such a lot to tell you,' she told Brian as she returned to the study. 'Shall we have a drink first, or coffee? It might pick you up. You look as tired as I feel.' He sat down heavily into the chair, telling her that he would have a small whiskey. She brought him the drink and sat down beside him, while she related what had occurred that day, the shock of seeing the photograph of herself still evident in her voice.

Brian stared at her, unable to take in what she was telling him. Why would anyone do such a thing? It's crazy, what reason could there be? 'You poor love,' he said shaking his head. 'It must have been a shock to you. Will this thing ever end? Let's have a look at the photograph anyway. It can't be as bad as you think.' She shook her head.

'Sorry, love, but I had to give it to the inspector. He is sending it for analysis.' Brian gave her an angry look.

'I would have thought that you'd have shown it to me first.'

'I did the first thing that came into my head, I phoned the police.' She thought that Brian was being unreasonable about it, but she was too tired to discuss it anymore that night. She told him that she was going to bed, feeling let down by his behaviour. Why couldn't he understand that she was frightened; she had never felt like this before, even during her divorce. At least then she had some control over what was happening.

It was the first time since they had met that a strained silence developed between them. They slept with their backs to each other, neither getting much sleep. Eva awoke to find a contrite Brian, coffee in his hand, smiling down at her. He put the steaming cup on the side table, and gathered her into his arms.

'Sorry, love,' he whispered into her hair. 'You have my permission to punch me if I ever do anything like that again.' Eva smiled as he tenderly undressed her. Their lovemaking was intense, each relieved that their disagreement was at an end.

Singing to herself, she showered and dressed in casual clothes, and joined Brian in the kitchen where the aroma of bacon made her feel almost giddy. She often felt ravenous after making love. Feeling fulfilled and happy, he held her tight, once again telling her what an idiot he had been. She kissed him as he left to go to his office. He said that he had a few errands to run which might take some time. She didn't mind, she had plans of her own. She intended to see her mother and stepfather.

They lived in the Cotswolds. She needed to feel the love of her family around her. Since David's death, she had been feeling vulnerable; she might have been with David when the car hit him. It seemed to Eva that life was just a game of

51

chance. David certainly didn't deserve to die; he was a good man doing a worthwhile job.

She had rung David's parents soon after the accident. The two women had become close and often had coffee together. She sighed; she could still hear the deep sense of loss in his mother's voice. Eva knew that feeling, when she had lost her own child all those years ago. The grief was always with you. She sighed and got ready to go out.

6.

Seated at his desk, chewing over what he had learnt, Marsh studied the photograph Eva had given to him. It was a normal snapshot; might have been taken by a mobile phone and enlarged. However, he knew that mobile phones were not very efficient when it was getting dark. Why was the photo taken? Was it a sudden whim; perhaps someone coming across a seemingly drunken woman, taking a photo of her, and then sending it to her for no other reason than some joker wanting her to know how she had looked?

He shook his head; the person involved must have known the judge well enough to send it to the court building. It seemed to him that it had been a carefully planned action, and one he was determined to get to the bottom of. He would like to meet the person or persons who had taken the photo; it was obvious that they had wanted the judge to look even more intoxicated, and with her clothes dishevelled as they were, she did look just that.

He remembered how upset she seemed when she had shown him the photograph... that and the fact that she was unable to remember what had happened on the evening Sharpe had been knocked down had taken its toll on her. He looked at the photograph again, wondering whether both incidents were connected. He reached for the phone and got through to the lab. He was anxious to see whether they had found anything which might clear up why the councillor appeared unwell when he was crossing the road.

'Can't say yet, old chap,' the cheery voice at the other end of the phone told him, when Marsh had inquired whether the results of David's post-mortem were ready. This only added to Marsh's frustration.

'Oh, why is that?' Marsh kept his voice level; he knew from past experience it didn't do to put these boffins' backs up or he would still be waiting this time next year. He wasn't, however, expecting the reply he got.

'We have a classified. Findings not to be released until further notice on this particular sample,' the man explained. 'From the top too. Know anything about it?' Curiosity had crept into the technician's voice.

Marsh tried to keep his voice normal. 'Sorry, can't tell you anything for the moment,' which, Marsh grimly thought, was true. 'Listen, I will be sending you over a photograph. Could you check whether it contains anything that might help us identify who sent it, and let me know as soon as the results are ready?' The lab technician said he would. Marsh put the phone down, his face thoughtful.

His boss obviously hadn't heard about the censure notice, or he would have mentioned it to him. He stared down at the file, searching for anything that might help him understand. In his experience, this particular action was rare; it could only mean that someone, perhaps the CID or anyone high up enough, had stopped the local police obtaining the results. Obviously they were unhappy with the findings of the post-mortem. As if in answer to questions going around in his head, the phone on his desk rang, interrupting his thoughts. He picked it up.

'Peter!' The superintendent's voice, sounded sharp. 'In my office now!' Marsh had no time to reply; the line went dead.

Two men sat in the office with his boss; they both stood up as Marsh entered. He eyed them keenly. *The long and the short of it*, Marsh thought as the superintendent introduced them.

'Peter, these officers are from Special Branch: Chief Inspector Givens,' indicating the shorter of the two officers, 'and Detective Blain. They have some information that will interest you regarding Councillor Sharpe's death.' Although his voice was quiet, there was an underlying gruffness which Marsh knew from past experience meant that his boss was not happy with the situation.

'Oh yes?' Marsh shook hands with the two officers. He steeled himself against the growing resentment rising in his chest. He caught the superintendent's warning look. Trying to choose his words carefully, but unable to stop the frustration he felt, he asked, 'It sounds as though you people know more than I, so can I throw a question at you? Why have you barred the results of Mr Sharpe's post-mortem from us? How are we supposed to reach a closure in this case if details are kept from us? I am the investigating officer. Surely I or,' he glanced sideways at his boss, 'the superintendent here should have been consulted earlier.' He saw the taller detective shift uncomfortably in his chair, but his partner answered, his voice smooth as though he was used to awkward questions being asked.

'Yes, Inspector, I can understand your frustration, but in cases like this…'

'Sorry, I'm not with you,' Marsh interrupted, 'in cases like what? Are you telling me that Councillor Sharpe's death was more than a hit and run?'

'Indeed.' Givens' voice held a smug note. 'The post-mortem on Mr Sharpe showed that he had a large amount of sodium thiopental in his system.'

Marsh gave a sharp intake of breath. This was the last thing he was expecting to hear.

Givens carried on. '6mg is a normal dose for a human. The deceased had double that amount. He was dead before the car hit him. We get involved when a barbiturate, only available under prescription, is a cause of death.' He paused to take a breath then continued, 'I don't know if you are aware this particular drug was used by the United States as part of their programme in the execution of prisoners. It anaesthetised them beforehand, although they do not use it now. It is used only under strict monitoring conditions and is carefully controlled.' He carried on talking, aware now that both the superintendent and Marsh were listening carefully. Marsh was used to events that were unusual, but this was new to him. His mind racing, he wondered why the Special Branch detectives had paid a personal visit to the station. They would know in time, he supposed.

'We have done a check on medical files in this area, clinics, any pharmaceutical companies that could issue this type of drug. We have had an in-depth look. I can tell you that according to all the investigations that we have followed up it wasn't prescribed or stolen by any medical establishment in this part of the town. We have looked at all the medical records, which leads us at Scotland Yard to the conclusion that people high up in the criminal world are involved.' He paused again. 'Police laboratories are authorised to inform us when results such as these turn up.' He folded his arms across his chest settling himself in the chair. 'This is an interesting case and one that Special Branch would be quite happy to take off your hands. We have the technology and know-how to get to the bottom of this case.' It was a long speech and the last sentence enraged Marsh.

'You are strangers here.' Marsh's protest was loud, all restraint gone. Clearly, he thought, this was the reason for their visit. Even though he hadn't asked for this assignment, he was buggered if he would let outsiders have it. 'You know nothing of the people involved. I have run my officers ragged in order to get results, now you waltz in...'

'Peter!' his boss roared, his face crimson. 'Shut it.' He turned to Givens, his voice calmer. 'However, I have to agree with my inspector, Chief Inspector. Despite his questionable outburst, he is good at his job, so with respect, we decline your offer to take over the case, and if need be I shall talk to your commissioner about leaving us in charge of it.'

The man from the Yard smiled, but Marsh saw that there was no amusement in his eyes. It was obvious to Marsh that Givens was not used to his suggestions being turned down.

'My chief constable will be in touch, sir.' He turned to Marsh. 'Your superintendent here seems to think highly of you, Inspector Marsh. I hope that you appreciate that. We will expect results soon. With that in mind, we are prepared to let you continue, with this proviso: that you keep us up to date with everything.'

Marsh agreed that he would, fully aware that his boss had put his neck out for him. He stared in surprise at his chief, gratitude mixed with a feeling that his boss's actions were probably not entirely for Marsh's sake.

'Anyway,' the Scotland Yard officer stood up, 'it's all in there,' he said handing Marsh a file. 'I don't know if you are aware that sodium thiopental, or sodium pentothal which is the common name used, is sometimes known as the truth drug. As I said, it is all in the file. Good luck.'

They shook hands again and left, leaving Marsh at a loss as to what to say to his boss. He managed a rather lame 'thank you' and knew that somewhere down the line his boss would claim a favour back. He returned to his office deep in thought. So the councillor might have been killed unlawfully. That opened up a string of questions to which he would have to find the answers. In the meantime, he had a free hand, and with the blessing of his super.

Back at his desk, he opened the file that the Scotland Yard officers had given him. According to the information inside, the councillor had been given or taken over 10mg of sodium pentothal. He would have died within minutes of taking it. This altered everything. If it was murder, and the inspector strongly believed it was, it meant he needed to set up a team. Deep in thought the inspector gazed ahead. Why had a man, seemingly at the top of his profession, died in such unusual circumstances?

'Bob,' he called, expecting to see his young assistant coming towards him. Instead he saw a slim dark-haired woman in a trouser suit stride up to his desk.

'Detective Sandra Pike, sir, I am Detective Todd's replacement.'

'What has happened to him?' he asked staring angrily at her. He had not been informed that Bob was being replaced.

He had got used to him; they seemed to work well together.

'He has broken his leg, sir, playing football.' Her voice had an edge to it. He supposed he had made it seem her fault. He smiled to lessen the impression of annoyance that he had given, and held out his hand.

'Sorry if I sounded a bit off, there is a lot going on at the moment.'

'I understand, sir. I read the file and I am up to speed on the case so far.' She handed Marsh a document. 'I checked the CCTV camera outside the Apollo; it was turned off that night. I had a word with the security chap. He was off duty on the evening in question, but he said that he had no idea why the camera should have been off.' She took a deep breath and continued. 'He gave me the name of the man who was in charge of security that night. He was only taken on a week or so ago, but when I checked the job he had done before, it was impressive. He worked as a security guard at one of the oil refineries, has a good record, name of Juanti Haig. I think that we can rule out any sinister motives where he is concerned. His English is poor. His mother was in bed when I called, a virus or something. Mr Haig told me that his mother had a relapse the evening of the lecture and he couldn't go to work because he was concerned about her. He had to call a doctor for her, she was so poorly. I have checked that out too, sir.'

'Thank you, Detective.' Marsh was impressed. 'What do I call you, when we are not being formal?'

'Pike will do fine, sir.'

Marsh felt that Pike would be an efficient replacement for Bob. She seemed to have covered all the points that he had been interested in. He filled her in with all the latest news that he had received from Special Branch. He handed her the photograph of Eva and told her to get it to the lab. He picked up the phone as she left.

The same lab technician answered. However, he was more forthcoming this time, obviously getting clearance to tell the investigating officer all the facts. In answer to Marsh's question, he maintained that the drug which killed the victim was newly introduced into the bloodstream. He was certain that the victim had not taken that particular drug before. Marsh agreed with the analyses. It did not make sense otherwise. Why take that amount knowing it was going to kill you just after an evening out?

He decided that he would have a word with Mr Sullivan; obviously Bob had not had time to check him out. He was the only witness at the moment to the accident that had come forward. Perhaps he might remember something new; anyway it was worth a try. He had to contact David's family first and inform them that their son's death was no accident. The pathologist had released the councillor's body for burial, so his family could go ahead with his funeral. Aware that what he had to say to them would be a shock, he took a chance that David's parents would be at home when he called.

Mrs Sharpe answered the door to his knock. He thought that she looked younger than he had imagined, although her eyes showed signs of recent tears. The clothes she was wearing were smart, and at the same time trendy. She had a bright scarf thrown around her shoulders; her hair, which was silvery blond, was cut short in a stylish manner. Marsh thought that her son, according to Eva, had probably got his charm and his flair from her.

She showed him into the front room, where her husband sat nursing a drink. He nodded to the inspector, his eyes concerned as he looked at his wife. Marsh accepted her offer of coffee and sipped it while he looked around the elegant room. On the sideboard were photographs of David and their daughter Stella, both looking young and carefree. The policeman thought, with some bitterness, how circumstances can change, with a member of a family so cruelly taken from them.

He noticed that the furniture was regal style, the room tastefully furnished, and as far as he could tell, no reproductions in sight; he thought also that it had a welcoming feel to it.

He turned his thoughts to what he had to tell them. He had always found it difficult to break the news of a tragedy which had happened to a loved one. He could have sent one of the officers who were trained in this kind of delicate work. He remembered, however, that when he had started out in the police force, he had had the good fortune to have an experienced officer to show him the ropes. One piece of advice he was given all those years ago, which he had never forgotten, was to treat all the people you come into contact with in your job with respect; you will find they respond positively. He felt he owed it to the dead man's parents that as the officer in charge of the investigation he should be the one to break the news to them of this latest development.

'I am pleased to be able to tell you that you are free to make arrangements for your son's funeral,' he said, hating what he had to say next to them as they clung together in relief over his words. 'Mr and Mrs Sharpe, I am afraid that I have more distressing news for you.' They were listening now, their eyes wide with apprehension. 'Your son died from barbiturate poisoning, by person or persons unknown.' Marsh carried on despite the gasp of horror from David's mother. 'We don't know yet how it was administered. What I can tell you is that it was not given intravenously, and only taken a few minutes before his death, probably in liquid form at the lecture.' Marsh had continued speaking, aware that David's mother was quietly weeping; his father, with a comforting arm around his wife, stared in horror at Marsh.

'Who would do such a thing? David was well liked by all. He had no enemies. You say a barbiturate was used to kill my son? What was it?'

'I am afraid I am not at liberty to tell you that at this stage, Mr Sharpe.' Marsh was aware that David's father had been a chemist before he had retired and would no doubt know the drug used to kill his son. 'I don't know if it will be any consolation to you both, but death was almost instantaneous. One of the angles that we are working on, sir,' Marsh told him, 'is that it could have been mistaken identity.'

Mrs Sharpe spoke up now, grief in her voice. 'How terrible that there are people about who would do such a thing, to think that my poor boy might have died for nothing.' Her voice changed to a firmness that surprised the detective. 'You must find out who did this, Inspector, and punish them severely, as we are being punished. Will you promise me that you will do that?'

'I will certainly do my best.' Marsh hoped fervently that his best would be good enough. He had decided that he would not question the couple regarding whether they had known if their son had taken drugs. He felt it would have been the wrong thing to do, when he himself was convinced that the councillor had not. He left the grieving couple, feeling depressed at such obvious pain.

7.

Akeem Sard glared at the man standing in front of him, fury showing plainly on his thin face. He was a small man with a sallow complexion, now red with frustration and rage. The Egyptian gave the impression of a larger man than he was, and he was used to having his orders carried out, which, until lately, had been the case.

'What the fuck were you thinking?' he asked, his voice shaking with rage. 'I told you to subdue the guy. Did I not explain to you, dummy? The police arrives, he's staggering all over the place giving the impression that he is the worse for drink, and bingo he's locked him up for the night to sleep it off. He would have been unable to put his case forward. There had been indications that the man at the council offices was not happy with the flats being built. Apparently he cared more about a bit of skirt than the money which the flats would bring in. We were in danger of losing the vote. That was what it was all about. He would have lost credibility. I don't kill people. That's not what I do.'

It was a long speech for him. His past life had taught him that it was not always wise to voice an opinion. Indeed it could have got you killed. He stared out the window, trying to stifle the rage that threatened to overwhelm him. He was not an advocate of violence, choosing to run rather than fight, but Sard was so angry at the man standing in front of him, he could have throttled him. All his carefully laid-out plans to get the councillor off the streets were now down the drain due to this man's carelessness – not only that, but the repercussions of Flint's actions may well have far-reaching consequences. He hoped this wasn't the case, but being a person who had lived by his wits all his life, he know that it was a possibility. He had to try and salvage what was left of the situation.

Adil Flint stood his ground. He was a big man, over six feet tall, and at a different time it would have been easy for him to overpower the older man staring angrily at him now, without any effort. However, Sard was his meal ticket. He knew that he had to tread carefully with his boss at the moment. His handsome face, with a goatee beard and with his long fair hair tied back, gave him an air of confidence. He knew the girls, even the younger ones, found him attractive. He took care with the clothes he wore, and liked to dress in all the modern gear. With the good money he earned from the man now glaring at him, he could afford to splash out on the clothes he liked. He smirked to himself; he was going places. He would put the bloke's death down to experience, and move on.

He remembered his early childhood spent trying to survive the grim realities of war-torn Bosnia. He had come a long way since first arriving in this country as a refugee with his mother. He had played rough in those early days, convinced that survival meant putting the boot in first. He soon learnt that his adopted country was different: no dictator here, or squalor. But he had no intention of returning to that way of life.

He knew that he had made a balls-up regarding the councillor. However, quick thinking had got him out of many a scrape before now, and he could do it again. He had always chosen the easier and safer way out of any hole. The fact that the bloke had been hit by a car was to his mind a stroke of luck.

'Boss, so it was a bit of a hiccup, I admit, but what was I supposed to do? The prick held on to his glass all night and only took sips out of it.' He shrugged. 'I had to think fast. The evening was cut short because the bloke talking was sick. Anyway, they think that your man was knocked down and killed by that stupid bastard,' he gave a snigger. 'He won't vote now.'

The veins on his forehead standing out with the anger he felt, Sard stared at Flint; the cigar he held in his thin hand shook. 'You fucking idiot, what you don't seem to understand is that I have to answer to people so high up the ladder they just have to raise their arm and you would disappear, me too. We are nothing to them. If they had wanted the bastard dead he would have been dead a long time ago. He was useful to us, as far as it goes. He is a hero now, and the vote is open again. Now I will have to rethink where we go from here.' Lesser men than Flint would have been intimidated, but he was still defiant.

'Well, what about the woman?' he smirked. 'With all your fucking planning, how come you forgot to mention that she would be tagging along?' Inwardly his boss conceded the point; the information he had received had been crap… no one was supposed to be with Sharpe. Not only did he take a companion with him, but it had to be the bloody judge. What shit he had been dealt, Sard thought bitterly.

It was a clever move, however, by Flint, to dump her in the park and take a photograph of her; yes that might prove very handy. However, he wasn't prepared to let this fucker know that or let him off lightly.

He had gone to some lengths to get that particular drug, because it would make a person appear as though that person was in a drunken stupor. He had paid good money for it too. He knew that he didn't have to worry about the authorities finding out where it had been obtained. He had bought it on the black market, from an unknown source, even to him... now he turned to Flint.

'So tell me, moron, how come she got the stuff as well? It was only meant for him?' Flint knew by the tone of his boss's voice that he was off the hook for the moment. He let out a deep sigh.

'I am telling you, boss, I only put the stuff in his fucking glass. I have no idea how she got hold of it.'

'You used too much. I told you that no more than 6mg was to be used. There is bound to be an investigation now when the cops find out that the car hadn't killed him. They will have to have a post-mortem. They will find out what he had been given.' Sard glared at Flint, waiting for his answer, aware that both of them were in a spot here. The people he was working for did not accept apologies; they issued orders, and expected them to be carried out.

'I was worried that he wouldn't drink enough to do the job. I had to put more of the stuff in as he was leaving, to make sure that it worked.'

'So you had to give him the whole fucking bottle, and I have to pick up the pieces. They are not too pleased, I can tell you. Your pay is going to be docked, and I hope that will be enough for them at the moment. Now get out of my sight before I really lose my temper.'

He was furious; fear of what their actions may be was mixed with anger. He had planned every aspect of the job that needed doing. On the face of it, it seemed a piece of cake. What could go wrong? He shook his head, what indeed? His instructions were straightforward: prevent the councillor from voting the following day. They would blame him; he knew that without a shadow of a doubt. He needed to think quickly; self-preservation was at the top of his list now.

8.

Eva decided that she would drive down to see her parents in the Cotswolds. She hadn't seen them for a couple of weeks now. She felt guilty, wishing that they lived nearer to her. On the other hand Sal, her sister, lived a short distance from her parents. If they were to move nearer, Sal would be in the same position as she was in. Her sister was married to Graham, who was a landscape gardener. He made a good living out of it and loved what he did, which was useful as he was able to keep her parents' garden in some sort of order. They had a son. John was a favourite of Eva's. She had often wondered whether, if her baby had survived, would he have looked like her nephew. Perhaps that was why she had such a soft spot for him. As his godmother as well, she had a special interest in what he did and where he was going in his young life. He would often ring her asking for advice on one thing or another. Eva liked the fact that he did this; it made her feel that he was somehow part of her.

On the way to her parents' she decided to call on Nikki. She hadn't seen her since that awful morning. God, was it only a few days ago? So much had happened in that short space of time. She wanted to tell her about the photograph which had been sent to her. Just another problem for her friend to worry about, but Nikki would go spare if that bit of news was kept from her.

Eva wondered if anyone would ever get over the loss of David – certainly not his parents or Stella his sister, of whom Eva was fond. They had become close and seen a lot of each other when she and David had first met. She knew that Stella would have liked her brother and Eva's relationship to have gone further than it had. After his accident, Eva had phoned Stella to say how sorry she was. Both women sharing the loss of David, though Eva was left feeling that her words were inadequate.

Nikki gave her a hug when she arrived and, with coffee in their hands, they made their way to their favourite spot in the garden. It was not only sheltered from the wind, but also wasn't overlooked by neighbours. Eva noticed that Nikki's eyes were red. But if her friend wanted to confide in her she was here, she knew that. Nikki had told Eva, however, that she didn't want to talk about it. Eva understood, and in answer to her friend's questions about her own news she told her all that had happened since she had last seen her. When she reached the part about the photograph sent to her at the courthouse and how dishevelled she looked in it, Nikki's face was full of anger.

'What sick fuck would do that? Was there a note attached, otherwise why send it? It must be blackmail, but why?' She shook her head in puzzlement. 'What does Brian think?' Nikki asked breathless after her rant. Watching her friend refill her coffee cup, Eva's eyes were thoughtful.

'Oh, like you, he is disgusted that anyone would snap me when I was like that. What sends shivers through me, Nik, is the idea of somebody standing over me making sure he got the most telling photograph. I rang the inspector and he took it away to see if any DNA could be found on it. I don't hold out much hope of that, but there's a chance that he might have been careless.' Eva sighed; where was that feeling of wellbeing she had felt before all this had happened?

'Let's hope it will all blow over soon. It might not come to anything. Then you and I, girlfriend, will celebrate by getting filthy drunk.'

'I don't think that I will ever feel relaxed about just enjoying a drink in public again,' Eva told her pulling a face. 'Too many bad memories.'

Her friend gave her arm a squeeze. 'Come on, girl, chin up, I am sure good times are coming for us all.' The last statement seemed to be heartfelt. Obviously, Eva thought to herself, Nikki's mind was on her own problems too.

'Amen to that, but already it is causing tension between Brian and me. I suspect he feels I am leaving him out of things, but it's not like that. He was annoyed that I didn't show him the photograph before I gave it to the police. Honestly, Nik, I was so shocked at getting that awful photo, I wasn't thinking straight. I just knew that I wasn't going to sit passively by and let some jerk blackmail me, or whatever else he is doing.' She took a long shuddering breath.

Nikki said thoughtfully, 'I notice you keep referring to the person as "he". Are sure in your own mind that it's a man. Why?'

'Yes, I know that I do, that's because I really can't see a woman standing over me, and adjusting my clothes to get the maximum view of my underwear. I could be wrong, but I just can't see it.'

'I suppose not,' Nikki agreed. 'On the other hand, women can be spiteful. Have you upset some woman and she is harbouring a grudge against you?' Nikki laughed to lighten her question. She could tell that Eva had lost a lot of her bounce.

'Oh, Nikki, thank goodness that I have you to listen to my woes.' Eva wrapped her arms around her friend, noticing as she did so how thin her friend had become. She had been so concerned with her own problems, she hadn't discussed her friend's. She chided herself, vowing that she would spend more time with her in future.

Saying a hurried goodbye to her friend, knowing that she had stayed longer than she ought to have done, Eva got in her car and she was soon on the M4 heading towards the Cotswolds where her mother and stepdad lived.

Their house was a charming nineteenth-century cottage built with Cotswold stone, which gleamed white in the sunlight. Her parents were at the door to greet her as she drew up, hugging her whilst drawing her into the cosy front room where tea was already on the table. At once Eva could feel a lot of the tension ebbing away from her. Her mother's gentle love and her stepfather's steadfast loyalty to Eva made her feel better.

Her mother and father had divorced when Eva was twelve. It had rocked her world and for a while her schoolwork had suffered; she became lethargic and difficult to manage, blaming both parents for their divorce. Eva knew that she had hurt her mother. Years later an adult herself, she looked back with regret at the way she had failed to understand that relationships break down, as she learnt to her cost. Her mother had never mentioned how hurt she had been by her

72

reaction. After a while, however, Eva had come to accept what had happened. She regretted also that she had seen so little of her dad afterwards. He had a new partner now and their paths didn't cross much; they were in touch with each other but on a casual basis.

When her mother had met Ted, Eva could never bring herself to call him Dad, even though he had been a more caring parent than her real father had been; he seemed to understand, and when her own marriage had ended in divorce, it was to him that she had turned. He was a retired barrister, and it was due to his encouragement that she had taken the bar exam. Glancing at her keenly now he remarked, 'You look tired, Eva. Been working too hard, love?'

'Probably, Ted.' She smiled weakly at him. She knew that she wasn't going to mention any problems she might have, but her mother said, 'Awful about David. Has the driver come forward yet? He was such a nice boy.' To her mother's generation, anyone under the age of forty was still young.

'Nothing as yet, Mum, but the police are bound to find him soon. Now tell me, what's been happening in your neck of the woods?' Eva was anxious to ward off any questions that she couldn't answer at this time; she knew that her stepdad kept a close ear to what was going on from the point of view of the law. He had lots of contacts still. She wondered whether he knew more about her affairs than he said. She could see that he was itching to question her more, but because he was the sort of person he was, he held it in. Instead he said, 'Sal and Graham said that they might drop in.'

'I hope they do, we have a lot to catch up with.' Eva smiled; she and her sister had always been close and Eva wanted to hear all the gossip. She glanced out of the window. 'The garden looks great, by the way. I must compliment Graham on the job he does. It is a pity he lives so far from us. Our little plot is sadly in need of attention.' She noticed a frown appear on her mother's face.

'How are Sal and Graham?' she asked. Ted, with a reproving look at his wife, reassured her.

'They are fine,' he said, continuing, 'What couple haven't got some problems? But it's nothing to worry about. You know your mother. Loves to worry about her girls.'

Eva's mobile rang; it was Marsh. 'Where are you, Eva? I need to talk to you. Your handbag has been found, cards and money all gone I am afraid, but I know that you will be glad to have the bag back, but first we are checking it for prints that may be on it.' Eva was aware that her face had shown some emotion, and that her parents were listening to what was being said.

'That's good,' she replied in a neutral voice. 'I am with my parents at the moment. I will phone you when I get home, thanks for that.' She noticed her mother's raised eyebrows as she put her mobile back in her pocket. 'Just a friend, Mum, nothing important,' then with a smile she asked, 'Is it alright if I have another cup of tea?', pouring herself a cup as she said it.

So her bag had turned up minus of course its contents, or at least any money or valuables. She wondered if they had found the person who had taken it; probably not if they were looking for fingerprints. She had no idea what Peter wanted to talk to her about. She became aware that her parents' house phone was ringing. Her mother picked up the receiver.

'I understand, dear,' she said replacing it and looking at Eva. 'Sal can't make it, Eva. She sends her love.'

'That's a pity. Never mind, I will phone her later, I am sure everything's okay.' Eva glanced at her watch. 'I have to go anyway. Sorry it was such a short visit.' Once again she felt the guilt that she had experienced earlier about living so far away from her parents. She knew that they didn't blame her. Mentally she gave herself a shake. *Buck up, girl.* In spite of all the bad things that had happened recently, she knew that she was lucky to have so many people around that cared about her.

She hugged them both, overwhelmed with love for them. She was reluctant to return home and back to whatever was waiting for her. Peter obviously had something to tell her, but that could wait. At the moment she didn't feel up to any more bad news. *Coward*, she thought, but then she straightened her shoulders. What was wrong with her, she wondered, giving up to negativity so easily?

The drive home seemed longer, she supposed, because she felt drained with fatigue with Nikki's problem still on her mind, and her own, and now perhaps Sal, though what was wrong there she couldn't imagine. They seemed to have everything they wanted. She was glad to arrive home. She knew that the stress that she had felt since David's death had made her more weary than usual. To her relief she saw that the lights were on. Brian was home. She drove her car into the garage space, and went inside. Brian was sitting in the front room, a coffee cup in his hand, reading a file which was open on his lap. He put the papers down and taking one look at her face, pulled a chair out for her to sit down, his face concerned.

'Has something happened?'

'Other than my bag turning up, no,' she told him shaking her head. 'It's been a long day that's all and I am truly whacked.'

Brian sat down next to her, his hand gently massaging her aching back as she told him about Nikki. He looked surprised. 'God, how does one explain all that to… how old are the children?'

'Beth is seven, Sara six. Yes, I know what you mean.' Eva felt that all the firm ground around their lives was disintegrating. It began of course with David's death. *Why is it*, she wondered, *that when we are happy, we don't always realise it. On the other hand we soon know when things start to go wrong.* 'Divorce is difficult for kids. I'm not sure how you can make them understand at so young an age.' She shook her head, remembering how she had felt at her own parents' divorce. 'Let's think of something else.' Seeing Brian's salacious look, she laughed. 'Down, tiger, what's in the fridge? I'm famished.'

9.

Inspector Peter Marsh had eventually got his team together. Like most law enforcement establishments, manpower was at a premium. He had, however, managed to acquire three good officers. He was satisfied that between them, they should be able to get some answers to why anyone would want to kill David Sharpe, and in such a way. He was, according to Eva, who was well versed in the way people behave, liked and had more friends than enemies, especially those who wished him harm.

Thinking of the judge now, he wondered why she hadn't got back to him. She still didn't know how Sharpe had died. He needed to speak to her again. Things had changed now; other angles would need to be investigated. One was why she was unable to remember anything after leaving the lecture and finding herself on that bench. Was it possible that she had been given something as well? It was a sombre thought that she too could also have died. Time was of the essence now to wrap this case up to everyone's satisfaction. If there was a killer about, he was determined to find him or her.

Now he looked over the list of his officers from the file in front of him. Top of the list was Sergeant Roger Smyth, thirty-odd years in the force, and due to retire next year. In normal circumstances, the sergeant would have been the obvious choice of being second in command, even taking over the investigation in the first place, but an accident during a heated demonstration had resulted in an injury to his left eye which had left him partially blinded. However, what he could bring to the team would be invaluable. It had been decided to keep him on so that his pension would be at a premium.

Marsh knew that he would be an asset to the team. He and the sergeant had worked together in the past. The inspector knew that the experience he had gained in those thirty years was useful; he had his ear to the ground and would be handy to have around. It was rumoured that he didn't want to retire, and would be dragged out screaming when his time was up. He was of the old school and would keep events on an even keel.

Next was the joker of the station, Lenny Myers. Marsh grinned when he thought of him. He needed watching, he wasn't the hardest of workers, but he had a quirky sense of humour, which helped when an investigation was dragging on without results, and he was a genuinely nice fellow, well liked by his colleagues. He was new to the station so was a little green, this being his first job since becoming a detective.

Last on the list was Pike. She had impressed him earlier. She would be a good replacement for Bob. Marsh had decided to put her in charge of the team in his absence, and take over if he himself was not available. Roger seemed to be quite happy with this arrangement. Marsh suspected that he was only too glad to be able to carry on in the job that he loved.

Marsh had the feeling that he had struck lucky with his team, especially Pike. Not, he thought, that he was glad that

Bob was indisposed, but he was feeling pleased at the way events had turned out. The main thing was that the team was well balanced.

They were gathered now in the small incident room which Marsh had managed to acquire. It was near to the office that he used. It wasn't the ideal place, too small to move around much. The main office was noisy, and at the moment was awash with officers investigating a gangland killing. He noticed, with some satisfaction as he glanced around, that someone had supplied a plug-in kettle, an assortment of mugs and a jar of coffee. *That should keep them happy*, he mused watching them talking among themselves.

Although they worked at the same station, the detectives had never worked together before. They were going to have to get used to the different way they each worked. *Should be interesting*, he thought. Opening a file, he withdrew several pictures and papers. Originally he had felt that he had been fobbed off with a hit and run inquiry by his superintendent, while the meatier one was being carried out next door by his colleagues. This had all changed now with the discovery that the man who was killed was no longer a victim of a traffic incident, but possibly had been killed by a substance which had led to his death.

Looking around now at the officers he had, he knew good work could be done here. The team were scrutinising files of the various facts gathered. Marsh coughed loudly to get their attention. They watched in silence as he told them the facts of the case. He had a board put up and was now adding names and pictures to it.

'What we have is a thirty-nine-year-old man,' he told them, pinning up the picture of a fresh-faced man who looked, he thought, much younger than his age. 'This is David Sharpe, a councillor, in fact an executive director of planning at the council offices, and apparently well liked. He was given a lethal dose of a barbiturate called sodium pentothal, sometime while he was at a lecture. We don't yet know how that happened. I have ruled out the possibility that the victim had taken the drug himself. There is no evidence that it was self-administered. It is prescribed as a medication for various ailments, albeit under strict control.'

Lenny interrupted him, his young face eager. 'Didn't Marilyn Monroe die from the same drug after she had taken it?' he asked. Marsh nodded, amused that Lenny knew this fact about this particular drug, but then, he conceded, the young seemed to gather information such as this as a matter of course.

'Yes, I believe so,' Marsh answered. 'It's a powerful drug, and the sooner we get to the bottom of where it came from and who had supplied it, the better.'

Marsh found it hard to understand why anyone would choose to kill a person with a drug like sodium pentothal. It would make the authorities very anxious to find out where the substance had been obtained. Scotland Yard had done a lot of the heavy work in that area although he would have liked his own team to have carried out the investigation as to who had supplied it, but that was that. He had to be content with it.

He was happy to rule out the establishments in the locality for which his station had responsibility, such as clinics, pharmaceutical firms, chemists and veterinary surgeries, and anywhere else that the drug could have been obtained from. What didn't make sense to him was that it would hardly have made a ripple if, as first thought, the councillor had been knocked down and killed by a car. He shook his head trying to tie it all in.

'Is it possible, sir, that it was an accident?' Pike broke into his thoughts. 'I mean, could it have been meant for someone else?' She felt Lenny's eyes on her, and she glanced angrily at him and was surprised when he nodded his approval at her question.

Marsh also nodded. 'Good point, it is worth looking at who else was there that might have an enemy or two.'

'Blimey, boss,' Lenny grinned, 'that should cover a whole lot of people.'

'Yes,' said Marsh, 'so why are you all sitting down as though it's a lazy Sunday? Get to it! Pike, you and Lenny check out the names of the guests who had been at the lecture. It's going to take some time, I know. We need to establish, however, whether there was anyone there who can't account for their movements after the lecture had finished or had a motive to harm Councillor Sharpe.'

Pike was on her feet, a file in her hand and an eager expression on her face. Lenny, however, rising from his chair said slowly with a note of complaint, 'That's going to take some doing, we don't know who they are.'

Marsh turned on him, exasperated. 'For God's sake, Lenny, you are a detective, that's what we do, we detect.'

Marsh had heard back from Forensics; no prints had been found on the photograph of Eva, which meant that they had been wiped clean. However, they had struck lucky with her handbag, which had been found behind a hedge in the park by one of the park attendants. There had been fingerprints all over it and according to the lab, the prints belonged to just one person, Eva's own prints having been taken into account.

As Pike and Lenny left the room to get the list of people who had attended the lecture the phone on Marsh's desk rang. It was the desk sergeant informing him that a Mr Thrombi was downstairs and would like a word in connection with Mr Sharpe's death.

'Right,' Marsh told him, 'put him in one of the interview rooms.' Telling the sergeant to follow him, Marsh made his way down the stairs, wondering whether this could be a breakthrough. He hoped so.

The interview room was stark and uninviting, which was deliberate; it had a table and a few chairs. The walls were a nondescript cream with the obligatory camera which left no one in any doubt what it was there for. When Marsh opened the door, he saw that the man was not alone; a younger man was with him.

'My name is Inspector Marsh,' he said, shaking hands with them both. When they were all seated, Marsh said looking at the two men, 'I believe that you have information regarding the death of Councillor David Sharpe. I am in charge of the investigation, and you are…?'

At this point, the young man started to rise, but the older man's firm hand on his arm stopped him. The boy was clearly nervous and looked ready to dive out of the door at any moment. It was obvious to the detective that he had been coerced into coming.

'Yes, Inspector, my name is Tiodo Thrombi, and this is my son Patrick. I believe that he has something to tell you.' The speaker was a tall man obviously used to giving orders. He was smartly dressed with a navy suit and a yellow-striped tie. His son was tieless but he wore a black blazer, edged with gold. Marsh tried to remember the university which had those colours.

'I…' the young man began in a faltering tone. His father laid his hand on his son's arm again.

'Tell the inspector, son, just what you told me.' Slowly the young man began again.

'I knocked down that man,' he said, then added quickly, 'It was an accident. I didn't see him until the last moment. Honestly, sir, I am so sorry.' He put his head in his hands.

'It is an offence to leave the scene of an accident, sir.' Marsh felt some sympathy for him, but asked, 'Why did you drive away afterwards?'

'I had taken my father's car without his permission.' The man's hands were visibly shaking. 'I wanted to impress a girl, and because of my colour, I thought that the police would give me a hard time.' All the time his son had been speaking the father had stayed silent. Now he said, 'I only found out about my son's involvement this morning, Inspector. I know my son has done a bad thing, but he is a good boy. What will happen to him?'

'That is not up to me, sir,' Marsh told him, 'but I can tell you that your son did not cause the death of Mr Sharpe.' Both the father and his son stared at Marsh then the son's face broke into a smile. Instantly the smile faded, as though remembering that a man had died.

'How did he die?' he asked, his voice still shaky.

'I am not at liberty to tell you that at the moment, sir,' the inspector told him.

Marsh questioned the young man further; he was

satisfied that the young man had not known the victim. If that was the case, it hadn't been a deliberate attempt to drive at the councillor and kill him. He glanced at his sergeant making sure this was all being taken down. *One loophole covered*, he thought, *but where does that leave us?*

The lethal dose could only have been administered at the lecture, as it was given to the victim orally, and according to the post-mortem, death occurred within minutes of drinking the orange juice that he had been holding on to all that evening. There was an urgency now to get the names of the people who were there. It took some nerve to put something in a drink with people about. He knew that Pike would do her utmost to get them whatever information they needed from whoever the organisers were. He dragged his mind back to the matter in hand.

'You mentioned that you wanted to impress a young lady,' he asked the young man. 'Was this young lady in the car with you when you hit Mr Sharpe?'

'Tell the inspector everything, Patrick,' his father told his son as he hesitated. 'Yes but…'

'Her name please, sir!' Marsh spoke sharply; he didn't have the time for niceties now.

'Her name is Coleen Daly, Inspector.' The boy's father spoke up. 'She is a nice girl. I hope this doesn't get her into any trouble.'

'We just would like a word with her, sir, to confirm what your son has told us.'

'But she won't be able to tell you much,' the young man protested, 'she was looking somewhere else.'

'I still have to talk to her.'

Marsh stood and shook hands with the two men. He

nodded to Roger to obtain the address of the other witness, and left the room with the girl's telephone number which had been given to him. He hurried back to his office. He picked up the receiver to speak to the young woman whom the father had mentioned. He was anxious to clear up as many loose ends as he could, bearing in mind that there were a lot more questions to be answered. He remembered then that Eva hadn't got back to him. She still didn't know how David had died; she still believed that the councillor's death had been an accident. With the phone still in his hand he rang her number.

'Hallo.' Her voice sounded slurred. 'Oh, Peter.' Her voice wide awake now. 'I dozed off. I didn't get back to you, did I? I'm so sorry. I seem to be apologising to everyone lately.'

'I need to talk to you urgently,' Marsh told her.

'Is it about David? Has there been a development?'

'Yes. Listen, Eva, when can you come down to the station?'

After a brief silence she said slowly, 'Now, I think. I will leave a message for Brian. Will that suit you?' Marsh knew that he had to talk to Coleen Daley... On the other hand, he didn't want Eva to hear how Sharpe had died from the media before he had a chance to tell her. She was going to be shocked as it was. 'Yes, that's fine. I will see you in a little while.'

She arrived half an hour later, giving Marsh just enough time to check on the whereabouts of his team. His sergeant was finishing typing up Patrick Thrombi's statement. The boy had left the scene of an accident, which was serious. Marsh decided to wait and hear what the girlfriend had to say before making any decision regarding charging the young man. He phoned Pike; a harassed voice answered.

'Sir, Lenny was right in saying it was going to be hard. With the list that the organisers have given us, we have, however, managed to rule out quite a few people, after checking them out, that is.' She continued, 'There were a handful of students, four I think, who were there having won the chance to hear the lecture because of doing well in their exams, and going up to Oxbridge. I have ruled them out as well. I will fill you in fully when we get back.'

'Keep up the good work, Pike.' Marsh grinned to himself. Pike would have her work cut out, not only following up leads but listening to Lenny complaining, but he knew that she could handle it.

Eva was dressed casually in slacks and a sweater. Marsh thought that she looked less like a judge than the other times that he had seen her. She had a wary expression on her face, probably, he thought, wondering what else he had to throw at her.

'Shall we go up to my office?' he said, leading the way up the staircase. As Eva sat down on the chair he held out for her, she glanced around the room. She thought how grim and airless the little room seemed. There were no windows and so much paper. Stacks of files were lined up on the table, in danger of toppling over. Her chambers had lots of papers and files, but nothing like this. She noticed too that there were no photographs on his desk; her desk, on the other hand, was covered in snaps of her family.

She realised that although she knew the inspector well, she didn't know an awful lot about his life. He had never married, she knew. She had heard that he lived with a widowed sister who kept house for him. He was obviously a career officer, she mused. She had no doubt that he would rise further up the ranks. She listened while he told her the latest development.

'I have to tell you that as a result of lifting fingerprints off your handbag, it has been found to contain prints other than yours and Mr Sharpe's whom you have told me touched it at one point.' Eva nodded, as Marsh continued. 'Unfortunately we are unable to release your bag at this point as it is evidence now.' She was uncertain whether to be glad about the prints or not; it might bring the thief to justice, but what about her bag? It had cost quite a lot; on the other hand, memories of where she had had it last would always be there to haunt her.

'I am afraid everything of value is gone.' He took a deep breath. 'There is something else I have to tell you. A strong barbiturate was given to Mr Sharpe sometime during that evening, which was the cause of his sudden death, and it was sudden, according to the post-mortem. He was dead before the car hit him.'

'No!' The cry was wrenched from her. 'That's impossible, how could that happen? I was with David the whole time in the room where the lecture took place, and as far as I can remember, he only had the one drink, and that was in a large glass, handed to him by the waiter. Did he have anything to do with it?' Eva couldn't believe what she was hearing; it was getting surreal. 'Why would anyone want to hurt David? Everyone liked him.' She looked at the policeman hoping that he had the answer. Marsh shook his head.

'We can't rule out mistaken identity. The waiter who

served the drinks – there was only one – has worked for the Cavendish Rooms for nineteen years. We have gone into his record. He is without doubt a person who in my opinion can be ruled out of the investigation.' Marsh picked up the phone and spoke into it. 'Can you come in here please, Officer?' He put the receiver down and turned to face her as the door opened.

As the policewoman entered, Marsh said, 'Judge Sinclair, I would like you to go with this officer. She will escort you to our medical unit. There the medical team will take a blood sample from you.' He held up his hand as Eva started to question him, still bewildered at the formal way he had addressed her. 'I will answer your questions when I get some answers.'

He was anxious to rule out something that had been bothering him from the start. Eva had stated that she had wine, while the councillor only had an orange juice. Someone had slipped a large amount of barbiturates into his drink, enough to kill him. He wanted to check whether she too had been given anything. If that was the case, why had she survived? He knew that it was very unusual for a person to fall unconscious after two glasses of wine. She had been quite certain how many glasses she had drunk that evening.

The waiter had been the main suspect in their investigations; after all it was he who had supplied the drinks to both of them. He had been, according to witnesses, very busy making sure everyone had a drink, which left plenty of time for an unknown person or persons to lace the councillor's drink. The more Marsh thought about it, the more he realised that it had been a well-thought-out plan. However, was the councillor meant to die? He wasn't sure.

They had ruled out the waiter because of his fine record... which left who?

On the other hand the judge might have been mistaken about how many glasses she had had. She may have had more than she had realised. He didn't believe that; he had always found her to be someone you could rely on to know what she was talking about, which left the other possibility: that her drink too had been laced. But what reason could there be for doing that? He scratched his head; more questions than answers. He was convinced, however, that it had all happened within that room. That one person – could be two or even more – had a hand in giving David Sharpe a drug which, taken in the amount supplied, had led to his death.

Eva returned from the medical unit looking shaken. Marsh couldn't blame her; a lot had happened to her and was still happening. He thanked her, and she left the station, a bewildered look still on her face.

10.

The funeral of David Francis Sharpe was held in a small, but well-known, church near to where his family lived. He had obviously been well liked in the small community because of the amount of local people who had come to show their respects. Eva was also surprised at how many of the people attending the funeral she knew from work. Obviously all of the officials and fellow councillors from the council offices were in attendance. Council business had been cancelled due to David's accident, including planning applications. Looking around, she saw people she came into contact with at the courthouse too. He had obviously been very popular, which made it even harder for her to understand why anyone would want to kill him.

She had gone there alone. Brian had apologised, saying that he would be locked in a meeting all that day. She would have liked him to be with her; he and David had got on well together. She knew that it was going to be a difficult time for all. She could well understand the trauma David's family were feeling: not only had their son been cruelly taken from them, now it emerged that it hadn't been an accident, but that someone had deliberately planned his death.

It was the middle of September, the sun low in the sky as she had driven to the small church. Normally she would have enjoyed the drive, passing well-tended fields with bales of hay scattered about. Now, however, she was still numb from what the inspector had told her. She couldn't believe it possible that David had been killed with… what was it called? Sodium pentothal? From what she knew of the drug, it was used to treat several ailments including epilepsy but not in the quantity given to David.

She was also puzzled by Peter's insistence that she have a blood test. What was that about? Was it possible that she too had been given the same drug, but if that was so, why had it killed David but not her? It would explain of course why she had been in the state that she had been in. She found it hard to concentrate on the funeral; the questions kept going round in her head.

She looked around. She was surprised to see Beattie, her law clerk, there. She hadn't mentioned that she would be attending when Eva had asked her to postpone one of the cases that had been due to be heard. She always had the feeling that Beattie had disapproved of David. Probably, Eva thought, because of his close association with herself. Beattie was protective of Eva and Brian's relationship, worried perhaps that David might have come between them. *No chance of that*, Eva smiled to herself, then a sob caught in her throat as she realised what her thoughts had been. David was no more.

Beattie was talking to the council's chief clerk, John Turner, whom Eva had never got on with, although she rarely came into contact with him, but the occasions that their paths had crossed, she had considered him to be small-minded. That could of course be because David had found it difficult to work with him. She noticed that David's parents and sister stood surrounded by family and friends. David's mother looked dreadful; she seemed to have shrunk since Eva had seen her last.

The service itself was simple, and quite short, Eva supposed because of the manner in which David had died. She wondered if the people gathered here at his funeral now had any inkling, other than his family and herself, that his death had not been an accident. The shock would be immense when they eventually find out. In the meantime, Eva wryly thought, David would have hated this low-key ceremony; his had been a larger-than-life personality, and this would have been too mundane for him. His sister spoke movingly of how she was going to miss him. Eva felt tears prick her eyelids, thinking that she too would miss his antics as well as his friendship; life would be a duller place from now on.

After the service, she watched as the coffin disappeared behind the curtain, taking what remained of her friend with it. Again she wondered who had hated David so much to want kill him in that way. She shivered, trying to understand the hate that had inspired such an action. It was too much to understand. David's sister approached as Eva was getting ready to leave; she had no wish to intrude on a family's grief.

'Eva, my parents would like you to come back to the house if you have the time.'

Stella, David's sister, was an attractive woman, younger than he had been. She was head at the local high school and, by all accounts, due to her teaching methods the school had received praise from every sector of the teaching profession. Eva smiled, thanked her and reluctantly followed the small convoy back to the house in her car. She would have liked to have just slipped away. She arrived at David's parents' house and was greeted by his mother. She gave Eva a hug.

'Dave was very fond of you, Eva. We had hoped that you might have continued to see each other, but life doesn't always do what one would wish.' Her face was pale and for a moment she seemed to sway, but she steadied herself saying, 'I haven't been sleeping well since…' She left the words unsaid as though they were too difficult to say, which, Eva thought, they probably were. She felt helpless against such grief. Stella approached her as she was thinking of quietly leaving. She put her arm through Eva's and led her aside.

'Let's go outside, the garden is lovely at this time of year.' Eva thought that David's sister probably wanted to know if she had been told more of the facts of her brother's death. 'I didn't want Mum or Dad to hear, they have enough to worry about as it is,' she said as they walked among the fruit trees, laden, Eva saw, with ripe apples. She saw that the garden indeed was quite lovely, and again she felt tears pricking her eyelids. David had loved to visit his parents, and it was he who had planned the garden. He had told her often enough how he had enjoyed working on it; it was so unfair. She glanced at Stella and saw that she too had tears glistening in her eyes. She brushed them away impatiently.

'I know that they will find the bastard that did this, Eva,' Stella said as they walked on in silence, then she turned to face Eva. 'I wanted to talk to you about David's row with Mr Turner.'

'I never knew anything about a row,' she told Stella, puzzled. 'Oh I knew that they never got on. What was it about?' she said, wondering why Stella was telling her. 'Apparently Mr Turner accused my brother of acting with bias. You do know that there is a large conglomerate behind the planning application, including some Russian businessmen? They have also put in for the same site that Brian wants for his centre.' As Eva shook her head, Stella carried on.

'No. Well they have. The planning committee meeting which had been due to take place the day after…' her voice broke, but she continued, '… the day after David's death. The two planning applications were on the agenda. David, as executive director of the planning department, expressed an opinion that the community project would benefit the whole community. It didn't go down too well with some of the councillors, including Mr Turner. I believe a nasty scene took place afterwards.' Eva still didn't understand why Stella was telling her this and said so. Stella pulled a face.

'Come on, Eva, surely you get what Turner was inferring? He thought that Dave was siding with Brian because of his fondness for you.'

'That can't be true,' Eva protested. 'Dave was too professional. He was the fairest person I ever knew.' Stella hugged her.

'Bless you for that and of course you are right. I wondered if it would be helpful to mention it to the inspector. I don't know how useful it might be.'

Eva said that she would, though what that had to do with what had happened to David she couldn't imagine. She knew that Stella and her family were desperate to find out who had killed David. She made her excuses and left, feeling guilty that she was so relieved to go.

When she reached home she saw that Brian's car was there. She was glad that he was home before her. She needed to feel his arms around her. He was seated, papers in disarray in front of him. He rose to his feet as she entered, his eyes on her pale face. She couldn't believe how vulnerable she had been feeling lately.

'Hey, love,' he murmured against her hair. 'It's okay.'

She told him about the funeral, and also about the row that had taken place between the chief clerk and David. She knew that what the chief clerk had intimated was nonsense, but what to do about it?

'Do you think that there is any point in my telling Peter? Surely it had nothing to do with what happened to David. What do you think?'

'Who knows. Tell the police and let them decide.' He shrugged, and then suddenly grinned. 'To change the subject, I have cooked for us. I think it's a mushroom bake, at least that's what it says on the packet.'

'Oh, you fraud, come clean, where did you buy it?' Eva laughed out loud, knowing that Brian was no cook and struggled with even the simplest of recipes.

'Okay, but I was still thinking of you.'

They ate their food in companionable silence, sitting side by side on the sofa. When they had finished eating Brian turned on the television. The newscaster was outside the local police station where a small group of the media was gathered. Superintendent Jim Townsend, his paunch more in evidence than ever, stood behind microphones being held out for him. He was clearly enjoying himself, smiling good-naturedly at those around him. Eva looked for the inspector.

She could see him standing in the background, looking decidedly uncomfortable as he listened to his superior outlining how the investigation was going. Superintendent

Jim Townsend always enjoyed talking to the media, and would, Marsh was sure, be most disappointed if what he was saying was not reported in the papers the following morning as well as on the local news. The media people liked him because of his willingness to talk to them off the record. There were a lot of questions being thrown at the policeman, who had just confirmed that it had turned into a murder investigation, and although he was doing a lot of rehearsed blustering, he wasn't giving much away, avoiding the awkward questions and promising to keep them in touch with any new developments which might arise. David was named as the victim. Eva felt ill hearing his name. It sounded so impersonal.

Marsh wanted to do his job without having to give away the few leads that he did have. He was annoyed therefore when the superintendent told the journalists gathered around that an early arrest was on the cards. Where that information came from Marsh had no idea, but it did put pressure on himself and his officers, as the media certainly would not let it go from now on.

His chief seemed happy at the way the interview with the press was going. Marsh noticed that his ego had been such that although Marsh himself had been standing near him and was the officer in charge of the investigation, his boss never mentioned him by name. However, Marsh was glad about this. He disliked the intrusion into the work being carried out by the police, and sometimes the media took it further, delving into a person's private life; they seemed to think it their right to do so.

He was anxious to get back to his office. He had a lot to do. He was bored now with the questions being asked. He edged slowly towards the door and was relieved when he was inside. He knew that he would be reprimanded by his boss for slipping away. He grinned; it was worth it not to have to listen to his boss's words which meant nothing.

He reached his office just as the phone rang. The call was from Eva who seemed concerned about a row that had occurred between David and Turner over votes. Marsh put the phone back in its cradle, looking thoughtful. What possible connection could there be in a disagreement over who votes for what? He looked down at his notes. He had already spoken to Turner, but Eva, whom he had just been speaking to, seemed to think that there was more to it than just a vote, or so David's sister had told her. He sighed; better not leave any questions unanswered. He knew that the council had voted on the two applications put in for the community and the luxury flats; it might be useful to know who had got it.

He rang the chief clerk, who reluctantly agreed to see him. He had taken Bob with him the last time; he would take Pike – *Let's see her take on things.* John Turner was just clearing away some papers when they were ushered into his office.

'Come in, Inspector,' he said, then as he noticed Pike added, 'You too, Detective. I thought that we had cleared up everything at our last meeting. Has something else occurred?'

'You heard of course that Councillor Sharpe was unlawfully killed,' Marsh began, settling more comfortably in the chair.

'Yes, quite shocking,' the clerk said shaking his head. Pike noticed as she looked around the office that the shredding machine had had a lot of use recently. She might mention that to her boss later, although it may not mean anything, other than Turner was not a paper hoarder.

'I believe that the council has already sat. I wonder, sir, what the outcome of the vote on the two planning applications was?' Marsh asked. Turner was slow in answering, still busy clearing away papers from his desk.

'I am afraid the result won't officially be made public until tomorrow, Inspector.'

'I realise that, sir, but it was a public meeting and this is a murder enquiry. I need to eliminate any suggestion that it might have anything to do with our investigation.'

'In that case, Inspector,' the clerk withdrew a paper from his file and handed it to Marsh, 'I can tell you that the planning committee endorsed the plans for the centre that has got the go ahead.' The clerk continued, 'The way planning applications are handled is complicated. Councillor Sharpe was Executive Director of Planning, and as such, in normal circumstances could have ruled without it going to a vote. In this case, however, he had decided to allow the committee to vote on it, although he had intimated that he would recommend the centre.'

'You thought that the reason behind his decision was personal, sir?' Marsh asked Turner who smiled grimly.

'I see you have been listening to David's sister, Inspector, but yes, as it happens I did believe that. What he had decided, against my wishes, as it happens, was wrong. I felt that the proposed luxury flats would bring in more revenue. I have no doubt that the planning committee would have voted against the centre for that reason. As things turned out, however, I suspect, because of the councillor's death, it seemed to turn the vote the way he would have wanted. Ironic, isn't it? If he had lived, the committee vote probably would have turned out differently.'

Marsh didn't know what to make of the result. Who had won? Mr Sharpe, but he was dead. Obviously Brian and his board were the winners, but apart from that, there didn't seem to be any underlying reason to kill Mr Sharpe over this. Another dead end.

Marsh went back to the station deep in thought. He had other things that held his attention. He needed to have a word with his superior about the young man who had hit David Sharpe and not stopped. It was a serious offence and normally it would have followed procedural guidance. On this occasion, however, taking in all the circumstances he was going to recommend that Mr Thrombi receive a formal caution.

This decision was an unusual one for the inspector to make. He hoped that the young man would prove worthy of his trust. He was also anxious to get back to find out whether Joe Quinn, the man who had taken Eva's bag, was in custody yet. Marsh wanted to clear as many things off his desk as he could, starting with Mr Thrombi. He went along to the superintendent's office to discuss the case. His boss looked surprised at the decision Marsh had made.

'Is that your university upbringing coming to the fore, Inspector? Would you still feel the same had it been some kid off the block with no prospects? To my mind Mr Thrombi broke the law. He left the scene of an accident, therefore he should feel the weight of the law behind him…'

'But he gave himself up, sir,' Marsh interrupted his boss, 'that must count for something. As to whether I would act differently had he been some other young man, I hope that I would treat each case as fairly as the law allows.' The superintendent's chair screeched in protest as he attempted to get to his feet, his face red with the exertion.

'You and your bleeding heart stuff. Off you go, and get me a result on the Sharpe case pronto.' Marsh phoned Patrick Thrombi explaining what was going to happen, cutting off the young man's thanks. He would leave it to the custody officer to issue the caution, knowing that he would put the fear of God into the young man. For his peace of mind, however, he had asked Roger to look into both Patrick Thrombi and Coleen Daley's background, just to make sure that they had not missed anything regarding the two young people.

11.

Eva walked along the corridor of the law court, her mind on the last two cases she had heard. She felt disturbed that more and more tenants seemed to be having real difficulty with paying their rents, especially young folk who were in arrears with their payments. As much as she sympathised with them, she was sworn to uphold the law, and act accordingly. However, there was a remit which allowed them to pay in instalments with as much as they could afford, and it was up to the courts to find a workable way for them to do so. She felt satisfied with the outcome of this morning's session, but now she was in need of a cup of coffee.

She popped her head around the door of Beattie's office. The aroma coming from within made Eva quite lightheaded. Her law clerk's coffee was undoubtedly the best she had ever tasted. Beattie was sitting behind her massive desk surrounded by files which littered the top of it. When she saw Eva she motioned her to sit down in one of the armchairs by the window. Two cups in her hand, she joined Eva by the window.

Her clerk was the one person whom Eva could talk to about the cases that came before her, and for a while they discussed one of the cases that Eva had heard and the conclusion and ruling that had been reached. She also had a court clerk who dealt with court work, but she valued Beattie's advice, aware that she knew the law backwards, researching and keeping Eva up to date with the latest developments of the law. She sipped her coffee, feeling the kick of caffeine as it entered her system. She leaned back against the chair; she had always felt at home in her friend's office. Her body was relaxed although her mind was still on the day's ruling, and the case she and Beattie had been discussing earlier. She became aware that her friend was giving her a questioning look.

'What?' she asked. She knew that look well.

'Don't tell me that you haven't heard, I mean about the vote?' Eva sat up.

'No, Brian went out early and you know that he never phones here. What happened?' She knew that Brian was counting on his project getting the council's vote, but there was a big conglomerate of wealthy businessmen who wanted to build a complex of luxury flats on the site. 'Tell me,' Eva demanded. Then, as Beattie laughed, Eva jumped up, almost upsetting the coffee she was holding. 'They did it!'

Beattie was not known for being demonstrative but she gave Eva a hearty slap on the back. She was a large woman, who ruled her department with the determination of one who knew how to get things moving. She and Eva had become close friends when Eva, a very green and newly appointed judge, had strayed unintentionally into the domain of the law which the clerk was responsible for. Eva had been set straight in no uncertain terms. After that, however, Beattie had been her ally against certain members of the bar which sought to denigrate her. This was mainly male initiated. They stood no chance against Beattie's tongue.

'They certainly did,' Beattie answered. 'It was a close vote, though the one thing which swung it eventually, or so, I was informed by John Turner, was the death of their favourite son. David was so popular with the other councillors.'

Eva was elated. Brian had worked so hard for this project; now his team could go ahead and plan the finer details of the centre. She waved goodbye to Beattie and hurried to her car with the intention of cooking something special to celebrate. Brian, however, was standing by the courthouse steps. He caught sight of her, and grinned.

'I can see that you've heard.' He opened the car door for her and then got in himself. 'We, my love, are going to celebrate in style.' It was so good to see Brian looking so buoyant again.

'What are you up to?' she asked laughing, thinking that perhaps now that the plans for the centre were settled, life might return to the way it had been, albeit she knew that the memory of David and the way he had died would stay with her forever.

'You and I, my darling, are going to grab a suitcase with some overnight stuff, and drive to the Cotswolds. I have booked a suite at the Empress hotel. I spoke to Beattie when I heard the news. She told me that you have nothing on for tomorrow, that is,' he hesitated, 'if you are not too tired?'

'Don't know the meaning of the word.' Eva grinned. She was impressed; the hotel was an exclusive one, and very expensive. Sal and Graham had used the same hotel for their wedding.

'Not only that,' he continued, 'I have arranged for your family to dine with us there tonight.'

'That will be lovely.' She was delighted that Brian had

thought to include her family. It had been a long time since they had all been together.

'We will have a great time,' he promised, and they did.

The hotel was one that was well known. It had a chef procured from one of the London hotels. The food was second to none, and Eva and her family made the most of the delicious meal. She drank far too much, trying not to think of the last time. She shook off the feeling, determined to enjoy the evening. It was good to see her sister looking so well; her skin, always the envy of others, was radiant, though Eva thought her a little quiet. She was touched to see Graham so attentive to his wife. John, their son, was allowed a small glass of champagne, which he drank down too fast and ended up coughing. Sal, trying to look cross but failing, mildly reprimanded him. It was also good to see her mother and Ted, both smiling contentedly at everyone. As she saw her family looking so happy, Eva offered up thanks to Brian who had planned all this; she thought that no matter what happened in the future she would look back at this as a magic time.

The view from their hotel window looked out over the Cotswolds. It was breathtakingly beautiful to Eva as she stood by the window later that night after her family had departed by cab, all a little tipsy. The garden was lit up by lanterns which hung all around. She realised what her mother and sister felt when they talked about this part of the country with such affection. Brian joined her, and together they watched the moon appear from behind the hills beyond, lighting up the whole valley. Eva knew that Brian felt the same as she. He put his arm about her shoulders.

'The view is something else, isn't it?' She agreed smiling happily up at him.

'Let's take a stroll around the grounds before we turn in. I don't want this evening to end.' She breathed in the scent of the flowers feeling Brian's hand tighten on hers.

Hand in hand they walked around the extensive grounds, the moon casting a bright light as they did so. They strolled along the path, admiring the well-kept flowerbeds, the past forgotten for the moment. It was mid-September now, but the warmth of the day still lingered. Eva was content just to be there with Brian. *Perhaps*, she thought again, *this is the turning point.* Brian getting the go ahead for the centre could be the catalyst for good times again. She hoped so.

Walking beside him, Eva could feel his inner excitement over the planning application success. Since they had first met he had always had a nervous energy, not able to sit still for very long. He held down an exacting job, which by all accounts he did very well. Although she had never met the other members of his board, the fact that they had allowed him to continue the project without interference told her a lot about how able he must be. They turned in at last, and despite the fact that she was reluctant for the evening to end, Eva suddenly realised that she was tired. Climbing the wide staircase of the hotel, with Brian's arm around her, she knew that she would sleep soundly that night.

12.

Akeem Sard stared out of his office window, a worried frown playing on his forehead. It had all gone to shit. He blamed Flint; if he hadn't killed the councillor, the vote would have gone the way it should have. It was a sympathy vote plain and simple, his man inside had said as much – that the majority of the council were in favour of the luxury flats purely because of the revenue they would bring in. Now they would have a centre where drug users and lowlife would gather, a drain on society. Who would vote for that...? But they had.

If Flint had carried out the job that he had been asked of him the councillor would still be alive but discredited and a poor representative of the council after being picked up by the police. Simple! He would have missed the vote. It was in the bag, or should have been.

Sard had rung the police to report the councillor's intended drunken behaviour, which also had turned out bad. He had telephoned the police switchboard just after eight when the talk was supposed to have finished, but the councillor was already dead by then. He had timed it all to perfection.

It had been reported in the press that it was ending at eight. That was another thing: Flint should have phoned to tell him that the talk had finished early. His excuse was that he had been too busy administering the drug. He sighed. Would anything go right for him? He toyed with the idea of leaving it to the company to deal with Flint. However, he had a strange regard for the man. He too had sought refuge in this country as he himself had; he also had to fight all the way to survive. He had come into contact with Kresnik Berisha, as Flint was known then, when the younger man had tried to overcharge him on a delivery he had made to his restaurant. The Arab was too clever for the Bosnian. When he had discovered the discrepancy he had threatened Flint with the law. However, Sard had seen something of himself in the younger man and had used him for various jobs.

Until now Akeem Sard had always worked within the law and his business acumen was without question. He owned several restaurants and the exclusive casino in the town. He conducted all his business ventures with care, and was above reproach, and if he had to admit it, he had been happier than he had ever been.

He had vacated Egypt, where he was born, in a hurry. At that time Anwar Sadat had been ruling Egypt for eleven years. Eleven years in which the young Akeem Sard had struggled to survive. However, when Hosni Mubarak had taken over after Sadat's assassination, Sard had suddenly found, with corruption everywhere, that he could make a lot of money buying and selling any commodity that earned him a profit. Life had been good all round. His bank balance had been very healthy. However, when Mubarak had been jailed for corruption, a roundup of anyone who had profited under his corrupt regime began.

The new administration was keen to seek out all those connected with Mubarak and make an example of them. Akeem Sard had to flee the country, fearing repercussions. He had transferred his assets to a bank outside Egypt, knowing that his funds would be confiscated if he had left them where they were.

He had managed, with a lot of his money handed over to corrupt people in authority, to obtain a British passport plus credentials allowing him to trade in the UK as a businessman. All this was unlawful, but he was fleeing for his life. He felt it warranted the actions taken to disappear from his country of birth. Once in the safety of Britain, with no blot on his character, he became a legitimate businessman.

All was going well until his world had collapsed. It came in the shape of a lawyer, who stood in his office one day. As he thought about it now, Sard was still at a loss how they had found him. He had covered his tracks well, but obviously not well enough. The lawyer had threatened to undo all Sard had achieved by exposing him as a fraud and an illegal immigrant. This threat had filled him with such dread that when approached by these people, he was forced to let them draw him into whatever they had planned. He soon found out what that was.

Working as their business partner they wanted him to represent them in obtaining planning permission for a new block of luxury flats in the heart of the town. He never found out exactly who he was working for, but the tone used left him in no doubt that he was dealing with ruthless people.

On the face of it, his role in applying for planning permission was legitimate enough. However, he had discovered that they were using laundered money to finance the project, money he suspected came from illicit drug deals, and quite possibly other forms of criminal activity.

He knew that he would do as he was asked; fear of exposure kept him awake at night, knowing that if he were to be sent back to Cairo he would not survive. All had gone well, until this added complication had developed. He was asked to find a way to discourage anyone else who was interested in the extensive area of land that the company had planned for their business venture. Now he had the worry of Flint's actions. He felt some kinship with him. It was Sard who suggested Flint change his name. The younger man had been working for him for quite a number of years now, and an uneasy trust had developed between the two.

He picked up the phone now, and dialled Flint's number. He waited as the call was transferred to another exchange then back to Flint. He didn't want his calls to Flint being traced by anyone. It was eventually answered by the Bosnian.

'There's another job I want you to do,' Sard told him. 'Get it right this time, otherwise I won't be able to stop them. If this goes well, there will be plenty of money in it for you. Meet me here in an hour. I will let you know what I want you to do.'

'Don't worry, boss.' Sard heard the greed in the other man's voice. 'The money is mine already, I have worked for you for a long time now. Have I ever let you down?' Flint's voice sounded confident over the phone, even though Flint could hear the threat in Sard's voice. He had got through more dangerous situations and people than these faceless ones his boss kept threatening him with. Sard could have explained what he wanted Flint to do over the phone. Ever cautious, Sard arranged to meet Flint at the casino.

An hour later, with Flint lounging in a chair in front of him, Sard spent the time outlining what needed to be done. As he emphasised the task that Flint had to do, he wondered whether he was putting too much faith in Flint's ability. He had to admit though, before this botch up, the man had done his job well.

Once Flint had swaggered off, his boss sat for a while, a worried frown on his face. The businessmen were leaning on him to get results. There was obviously a lot of money involved. He disliked what he had told Flint to do, but fear was a great leveller. He lit up a cigar and sat thinking. He wasn't young anymore; he realised that he was tired of the constant pressure put upon him by the company. More and more he had come to realise that they would stop at nothing.

Sard himself had never killed anyone or ever wanted to. He regretted the unfortunate death of the councillor. It shouldn't have happened. He wondered if his bosses had the same sentiment. The tone of the contact in Cairo held threats that seemed to hold no bounds. His life here as well as in Egypt was on the line. It was time to get out. He had decided this some time ago, and had started to wind up his business interests in this country. He had to accept a much lower return for them all. He sighed. Profits from the casino were big; he regretted the fact that he had to let that go; he did so hoping that no leak of his intentions would get back to the company.

Once this job was successfully over – he didn't even contemplate failure – he would get away somewhere. With the money that he had been promised, he would be able to afford to go to any country he chose. He gave a sigh and settled back in his chair and lit another cigar.

13.

Inspector Peter Marsh sat in the incident room, surrounded by files. He had been going through them, intent on finding anything that he had overlooked. His team had been busy; he had seen little of them since that morning. They had gradually filed into the incident room and now sat around the table, the hum of conversation sounding loud in the small room.

'Okay, settle down. What have we got so far, Pike?'

'You will see, sir,' she said handing him a file, 'that we have covered as much as we could. Of the fifty-odd people who attended the lecture, we have ruled out most of them. We still have a few more to check out. Of the ones that are left, Lenny and I have shortlisted the people that we think bear another look.'

'Thank you, Pike, you too, Lenny. It couldn't have been easy to separate the people who are of interest to us.' He turned to Roger. 'Sergeant, what have you found out about the witness who ran his car over the deceased?' Marsh asked, aware that he had already made a decision about that.

'Well, sir, first off, I checked the family. No previous on any of them. The father owns his own business. They are all well thought of especially the son who has won a place at Oxford.'

'Has he now?' Marsh said, impressed. A mark on his record now would be damaging to him; on the other hand, his super would have a field day with that information.

'Coleen Daley, the girlfriend – good family, no previous,' the sergeant told him. 'She had met Patrick Thrombi at his graduation, when a relation of Miss Daley's had his graduation at the same time. They have been going out together since.' 'Thank you, Sergeant, well done, all of you. I have some news which will interest you. The substance which killed Councillor Sharpe has also turned up in Judge Eva Sinclair's bloodstream. The lab can't say for definite what the amount of the dose taken was, as it was some days ago. Obviously not enough to kill her, just enough to make her senseless. We now have the job of discovering how it got into her system.'

Marsh was pleased to see his officers all taking notes; even Lenny, his tongue out in concentration, was scribbling away. Over the years that he had been running his department, Marsh had known many officers and learnt how they worked, some good, others not so. In his opinion the team he had now was hardworking and one of the best he had worked with... not that he was going to tell them that, and although he hadn't wanted this assignment, it was developing into an interesting case. Of course he regretted that a man had died, but the fact still remained he was enjoying the investigation.

'The other bit of news that we have is that the prints on Judge Sinclair's handbag match a small-timer, name of Joe Quinn. I have asked the uniform branch to go and bring him in, if they can find him. In the meantime,' Marsh said looking at Pike, 'I want you and Lenny to carry on eliminating the people who were at the lecture.'

He waited for Lenny to object, but to his surprise he nodded his agreement. As the two of them left, Marsh turned to his sergeant. 'What was that about? I expected Lenny to start complaining again.'

'Ah, sir, love's own dream,' Roger told him. 'He is love struck. Didn't you notice how he hung on every word Pike uttered?' Marsh didn't, but if it got results… He told Roger to grab his jacket.

'You and I are going to have a word with Coleen Daley, the young man's girlfriend. I also want to talk to Val Sullivan again. They are both witnesses. I am hoping that they will have something of interest to tell me.' Marsh hadn't been surprised when the lab had revealed that Eva had the same barbiturate in her bloodstream; it was the only possible explanation of why she blacked out suddenly. It was fortunate that it was still in her system. He knew that Eva was going to be shocked. He would wait until he had spoken to Ms Daley before getting in touch with the judge. She was a strong person, but this latest piece of news on top of everything else might be too much for her.

Coleen Daley was an attractive young woman. She wore no makeup and Marsh noticed that she had a sprinkling of freckles on her nose. She gave the officers a ready smile, but Marsh saw that she was nervous. They were seated in a bright cheerful room; coffee was laid out before them with what looked like homemade fruit cake which Marsh hadn't tasted since before his mother's death. He saw that his sergeant was helping himself to a slice. Plates and the coffee were handed out to them by the girl's mother, who to Marsh's eyes didn't look much older than her daughter. She left the room, closing the door silently behind her with a reassuring glance at her daughter.

'We won't keep you long, Miss Daley. I expect that you know why we are here?'

'Yes, Inspector,' she nodded, 'Patrick phoned me. I hope that was okay?' She looked uncertainly at both of the detectives. When Marsh reassured her, she continued. 'After it happened, Patrick was so scared. I begged him to stop, but he panicked and kept on driving.' Marsh wasn't very good at putting witnesses at ease. He glanced across at his sergeant.

'Yes, we have Mr Thrombi's statement, Miss Daley, you have nothing to worry about.' Roger smiled at her. 'However, we need to take a statement from you, just for our records.' He finished quickly as he saw her face fall.

'But I honestly didn't see anything. I was looking somewhere else. I only realised what had happened when I heard that dreadful noise.' She shuddered as she remembered the impact on the car.

'I am sure that it was upsetting for you, but why didn't Mr Thrombi see Mr Sharpe? I believe that the road was lit up that time of night.' Marsh was dismayed to see tears forming in the girl's eyes.

'It was my fault, you see, I called for him to look at something else, and that's when it happened. If only I hadn't done that, the poor man would have been alive.' Marsh had always felt uncomfortable when witnesses became emotional. He felt that they were getting nowhere. He reached hastily for his coat, and rose to his feet.

'Mr Sharpe was dead before the car hit him, but Mr Thrombi should have stopped.'

The girl got to her feet and followed the two police officers along the corridor. Her mother was waiting for them, her eyes anxious as she opened the door for the two detectives.

'Is everything alright now, Inspector? Coleen is not in any trouble is she?' She put an arm around her daughter. 'She shouldn't have distracted Patrick when she asked him to look at the drunken woman crossing the road. He wouldn't have taken his eyes off the road had she not…'

'What drunken woman?' Marsh interrupted, his voice sharp. He had already stepped out of the house, but now he paused and turned back to the two women.

'There was a woman so drunk that she had to be helped across the road by a friend. Patrick turned to look at what I was watching, just as I felt the car hit something.' The girl was openly crying now.

'This man that you say was helping the woman across the road, did you get a good look at him?' Marsh asked. 'I am not sure. I was too interested in the woman, who just could not stand up,' the girl told him drying her eyes on the handkerchief that her mother had handed to her.

'Can you describe the couple?' Marsh asked. This altered everything; there was now a witness who probably saw Eva when she came out of the lecture.

'I didn't notice much about her or the man. She had fair hair that I do remember; it had fallen across her face. I remember that she had on a blue dress, I think. It was getting dark so I am not too sure about that. I wasn't looking at the man. Is it important?'

'It might be. I would like you to come down to the station and make a statement.' He would ask one of the team to oversee that and to show her some pictures to see whether she might identify anyone. Marsh and the sergeant left, feeling satisfied, another piece falling into place, he thought. At least he imagined that the woman was Eva, though who the man was, he had no idea. It certainly wasn't David Sharpe; the poor devil was by all accounts already dead by that time. If not dead then certainly dying.

He now had the unpleasant duty of informing Eva that she had had a narrow escape. Forensics had told him that she had only a minute dose of the substance that had killed the councillor, which in normal circumstances would have had little or no effect on her. However, with the intake of alcohol as well, it is known to accelerate in the bloodstream.

14.

Eva was making a special dinner for them both. It was a kind of celebration: the fact that Brian now had the plans for the centre endorsed and she and Brian had been together for six months, and although they had the occasional hiccup, their relationship had developed into a warm and caring one... Apart from the last few days when David had died, she had been happier than she had been for years. She found herself warming to the idea of becoming Brian's wife. She knew that it was what he wanted; they loved each other and the doubts that had been in her mind were quickly receding.

She hummed as she cooked, wryly aware that she wasn't the superb cook that her mother was, but then her mother had chosen to spend her life at home raising her children, cooking, and caring for her husband. A lot of good that had done her, Eva thought bitterly; her father had quickly found an added interest in his young assistant; not quite the same as Eva's experience, but similar enough to know how devastating it must have been for her mother. She shook away her grim thoughts, determined to make this an evening to remember. She was about to call to Brian, who was in the study, to tell him dinner was almost ready, when the doorbell went. She was annoyed at the intrusion and opened the door.

'Inspector,' she said, hoping that her voice sounded more welcoming than her thoughts. He quickly apologised for the lateness of the hour as he followed her into the front room.

'It's rather urgent that I talk to you tonight. I wonder, is Brian here?'

'Yes,' she replied wondering what he wanted.

'I would like to talk to you, Eva, and if Brian is around he will want to hear it as well.'

'Why would that be?' Brian had heard the last part that Marsh had said; the inspector turned to face him.

'I was just apologising to the judge here for interrupting your evening.' He took out a file and laid it on the table in front of him, and with pen in hand began to write. Eva gave Brian a worried look.

'What's happened?' she asked as Brian put his arm around her.

'This is for the record, so I have to be formal,' Marsh told them. 'Judge Sinclair, I have to tell you that a substance was found in your bloodstream, which when tested proved to be sodium pentothal. Have you any idea how it came to be in your system?'

'Look here,' protested Brian, 'you can't barge in accusing Eva of… what, taking drugs?'

Eva smiled at Brian's shocked expression. She was familiar with the way police jargon went. At the same time she too was shocked at what the inspector had said. She answered carefully, aware that it would be on record.

'I have no idea, Inspector. Let me understand, are you telling me that someone laced my drink as well as David's? Why am I still alive then?'

'I can't tell you that at the moment. However, cast your

mind back. Is there anything that you may have remembered since we last spoke? Did anything happen that might help us in this investigation?' Marsh looked at her searchingly. She began shaking her head, but stopped as her face cleared.

'Oh my God, Peter,' she said, forgetting to be formal, 'I recall now that when the lecture was cut short, and we were ushered out of the hall. David had some orange juice left in the glass he was still holding. It must have been about half full. He said that he couldn't drink it all. He offered it to me and I took a couple of mouthfuls. David drained the glass. Surely the small amount I drank was not enough to affect me?' Eva shook her head in bewilderment.

'Not ordinarily, but when taken with wine,' Marsh smiled grimly, 'it apparently escalates in one's system. You were lucky that it wasn't enough to be fatal. At least that clears up how it was that you received a dose.' He rose. 'I will need you to sign this, once it has been typed up. Again I am sorry for the intrusion.'

As the door closed behind him, both Eva and Brian stared at each other, all thoughts of dinner and celebration gone from their minds. He still had his arm around her; now he tightened his grip, unable to contemplate what could have been the outcome had Eva taken more of the barbiturate. All the news about the planning application forgotten, he realised how much he loved her. To think that he might have lost her was beyond imagination. He looked at this woman before him wishing that he could wrap her in cotton wool to protect her from any danger which had taken her friend.

15.

Val Sullivan lived near the police station. The inspector realised then what was so familiar about the man's name: he was the janitor at the station. Marsh had recognised him as soon as they met, and the brief statement that was taken originally, at the scene of the accident, was by one of the officers from the uniform branch.

'Mr Sullivan, my name is Inspector Peter Marsh. I am carrying out the investigation into Councillor David Sharpe's death.' Marsh spoke formally because Roger was taking notes. He noticed the janitor's smile at such an official tone, as they had often shared small talk and a cup of coffee in passing at the station. He continued, 'I believe that you witnessed the accident on the evening of 10 September, is that correct?'

'That's right, Inspector,' the man said adopting the same tone. 'I had been to the lecture, but it ended suddenly due to the professor feeling unwell. When I got outside, the crowd seemed to have gone, cos I had to go to the lav, didn't I. Anyway I noticed that the judge, I mean Ms Sinclair, was swaying. She seemed about to fall. I grabbed her. As I did so, I looked around to see if there was someone to help. I noticed a man staggering across the road, going all over the place, he was.'

'What happened then? What about Judge Sinclair, was she conscious at that time?' asked Marsh, aware that police first on the scene at the time had already got a similar statement. It was good practice, however, to run through it again in case the witness remembered something new.

'When I saw what was happening I left Ms Sinclair leaning against the wall and rushed to see if I could help. The judge didn't seem to know what time of day it was. She looked dazed as though she'd had a skinful.'

'Did you recognise the man you saw staggering across the road, by any chance?' Marsh asked trying to get as much information from the janitor as he could. He was the only witness to come forward who had actually seen the councillor crossing the road, apparently to get his car, which, the police found, had been parked there.

'Oh no, never seen him before. Now the judge, I knows her, she sorted my girl out when she had that accident. Did alright by her too. I would recognise her anywhere.'

'Mr Sullivan, think carefully before you answer, did you see what happened to Judge Sinclair? Was there anyone near you when you helped her before the accident happened?' Sullivan shook his head.

'Naw, there were people about, course there was, but by the time I had done what I had to do, they didn't hang about. I didn't notice anyone in particular,' the man said shaking his head. 'They all seemed to be in a hurry.'

'Yes I understand that, sir. What happened when you got back to Ms Sinclair?' Marsh asked.

'I didn't go back.' The janitor stared. 'Blimey, a bloke had got himself killed. I didn't have time for anything after that. The Bill was there in no time, quicker than I have ever seen them, and I had to give them a statement.

Marsh thanked him, and the two policemen left. Marsh was disappointed; he had hoped that the janitor would have remembered something else. He hoped that they would get a lead on who it was that had taken Eva to the park. On the other hand, he was glad to know that the janitor seemed to be clear in what he had seen. It was always helpful to have a witness like that. He phoned Pike on his mobile.

'Did you get the information we wanted?'

'I got all the statements from the rest of the people at the lecture, a couple of interesting ones too.' She sounded upbeat which made Marsh hopeful that she had discovered something important.

'Did you ask them if they had seen either Ms Sinclair or Mr Sharpe outside the hall after the lecture?'

'Yes, unfortunately no one seems to have seen them other than in the hall, where a Mr and Mrs Chambers said that they sat next to them, but they didn't linger afterwards. Same goes for the others that I spoke to. They had gone before the accident. Sorry about that, sir, however, they did confirm that Mr Sharpe held on to the same glass of orange juice all evening.'

'Good work, Pike. I will see you back at the station later.' Marsh put his mobile away and filled the sergeant in with what he had just learnt. 'It looks like everyone did a disappearing act after the lecture. We only have one eyewitness who saw Ms Sinclair with Mr Sharpe. Sergeant, will you have Miss Daley brought to the station? Show her some mugshots of people known to us, and also show her a photo of Ms Sinclair. But first see if you can get an identikit going of the man and the woman that she saw.

Who knows, we may get a break. I want to know what Pike and Lenny have for me. She seemed to think that it might be important.'

Marsh reckoned it would take the sergeant a couple of hours to show Ms Daley the photographs of people known to the police. With a bit of luck she might recognise someone who had a record. He ate a sandwich at the local café, his mind full of what he had to do. So far, Joe Quinn had evaded the police. He lived in a squat, and was never around when the police called, but they were keeping an eye on the squat where he lived.

Lenny had his feet up on the desk when Marsh arrived back to the incident room. He quickly removed them when he saw the inspector. Pike was busy typing her notes up; Marsh was impressed at the way her fingers flew over the computer and told her so.

'I took a secretarial course before I finally settled for the police force,' she grinned. 'I thought that I might try my hand at office work.'

'Glad you changed your mind, Pike,' he said thinking that the more he saw how she worked, the more convinced he became that she was sure to go up the promotion ladder. She did detective work in an easy but efficient manner which got results. 'Let's hear what you two have got!' Pike took her notebook from the table.

'We spoke to most of the people at the lecture. The ones we didn't get to talk to either didn't live in this country or were on holiday when they went to hear the professor talk. The rest were very elderly and had a rented car waiting afterwards.' She took a deep breath. 'We ran data on them. All of them checked out, except two. Both had some priors.'

She read from her notebook. 'Mr Sam Holland, thirty-two, lives in Lime Street, went to the lecture with his girlfriend, been had up for possession eight years ago, nothing since.'

'Who is the other one?' Marsh saw that Pike's eyes lit up. He knew that she and Lenny had had their work cut out. They must have worked through the night to eliminate all except two.

'Mr Adil Flint, forty-two, gives his address as Cambridge Gardens. We haven't checked that yet, had quite a busy day, and night,' she added with a yawn. 'The interesting thing about him is that Adil Flint is not his given name. He came into this country as a refugee in 1987, from Bosnia. Changed his name from Kresnik Berisha in 1997. Lenny ran a check on that name and guess what came up? Drugs, scams, in fact you name it, and you'll find the young Adil in it somewhere.'

'That's interesting. On the other hand, coming from Bosnia, and all that horror, I wouldn't blame a youngster going a bit wild. Well done. We need to talk to both of them.' Marsh was pleased; the two detectives had worked hard and he told them so, adding, 'I'll get someone to bring Mr Flint and Mr Holland up on computer, maybe Ms Daley might recognise one of them.' He looked at his watch. 'Get off home now, we will see you tomorrow.' He felt that the investigation was moving along in the normal fashion of checks and interviews. Once all that was done he needed to sum up all the evidence to see where it was leading. He wasn't at that point yet, but it was going to plan, as long as he could keep the super off his back.

16.

Eva arrived at the courthouse early, feeling refreshed after spending a leisurely evening with Brian. They had drunk too much wine and laughed a lot and had played Scrabble. Brian had been in one of his playful moods, making up ridiculous words telling her that they were correct; Eva had collapsed in laughter. It had felt so good. Eva was grateful to him; she knew that he was trying to help her forget about David and the information the inspector had given them. In the courtroom, she heard a couple of motor offences before lunch.

She finished the cases and was back in her office when her mobile rang. It was her sister. Eva almost hugged the phone, thankful that she had turned it on earlier when she had finished hearing her last case. She was so glad that Sal had phoned her. She had been thinking of phoning her if she had not heard anything.

'Hi love,' she said. 'How's things?'

'Oh you know, so so. We all had such a nice time the other evening, thank you so much. It was special, wasn't it? Even John said how cool it was.' Sal carried on, 'Listen, Eva, any chance you have a free moment? I wondered if we could meet?' Eva looked quickly through her timetable.

'I am free around four, would that suit you?' She could hear the relief in her sister's voice.

'Great, I'll see you outside at four.' Sal hadn't known David except in passing. Eva decided that she wouldn't mention anything about the drug; it would only get back to her parents. Eva was puzzled; it was a long way for her sister to drive so late in the day. She wondered whether things were alright. She hadn't paid much attention to her mother's worried expression, but thinking about it, Sal had been rather quiet when they had all gone out to the hotel. The sisters hugged when they met and Eva suggested a little bistro not far away.

'Oh I'm not hungry,' Sal protested.

'Wait till you have tasted their sun-kissed tomatoes with olives, and slivers of bread. Delicious!' Eva replied, slipping her arm through her sister's as they walked along the road.

'Eva, you are so much part of all this,' Sal said indicating the busy traffic and the people hurrying along.

'I suppose I am. It's not your scene though, is it?' Eva and her sister were worlds apart in most things. After their parents' divorce, while it had ripped through Eva's security and left her feeling abandoned, her sister had thrived, going on to university, gaining a first in business studies and art, then setting up as an interior designer, with a clientele of loyal followers, all done within a few miles of the Cotswold hills. She had met and married Graham, and when their son had come along they had bought a plot of land and a couple of horses. It sounded idyllic, and it was, but not for Eva, who loved the noise of a busy city. Seated at the bistro, the two sisters sat facing the window. Eva let the companionable silence draw out whatever her sister had on her mind. What she did say made Eva sit up; it was so unexpected.

'Eva, what was it like to lose your baby?' Eva stared at her sister trying to gauge where this was going. It was so long ago, but she had to be honest.

'It was the most awful experience I have ever had in my life. Not only was my body damaged, but in some ways my mind was too. Stephen and I were in love, or I was, and I thought that nothing could happen to destroy our wonderful life. I believed that he was happy. When I found out that I was pregnant, it seemed that a child would complete our life. I dreamed of having our little baby. It was not to be.' Eva related this dry-eyed, but Sal had tears in her eyes.

'Oh, sweetheart, you went through so much, and I wasn't there for you. Forgive me for being so selfish.' She threw her arms around Eva, tears running freely down her face. Eva was startled at her reaction.

'Hush, love, you were so young. What's going on, Sal?' Aware now that the other diners were beginning to take an interest in their conversation, Eva put a hand on Sal's arm, not only to comfort, but to stop her sister from becoming too emotional.

'I'm pregnant,' her sister wailed. 'What am I going to do?'

'That's great news, Sal,' Eva laughed with relief. 'Give John a companion. What does Graham think? Is he happy about it?'

'Oh he is all for it. I am thirty-six, Eva. I have just got my life together. How can I start all over again? What's going to happen to my career?'

'Nothing is going to happen to your career, Sal, babies fit in. It's not as though you have a structured life. You'll be fine.' Eva was thinking what she wouldn't give to be in her sister's shoes: have a husband who loved her, a baby to complete it, albeit not in the country, but otherwise it would be perfect. All the past came flooding back and for a moment she was unable to speak. She pulled herself together.

'Have you told Mum and Ted? They are really worried about you. You know, Sal, you have the perfect babysitters, they would just love to have a baby to look after, it will be wonderful.'

'You think so?' her sister said doubtfully. 'It is going to be a big adjustment, but I suppose it would be nice to have a little baby around again. Hey! Perhaps it will be a girl. Graham always said that he would have liked to have a girl. Not,' she hastened to add, 'that he was disappointed when John came along.' Her face cleared. 'I suppose you are right. God, I feel so much better talking it through. Thanks, Eva, for putting up with me.'

'I haven't done anything,' Eva protested.

'Oh yes you have. Just having someone to listen and not judge is great. I am going to tell the parents. You are right. I remember how Mum seemed to come alive when she was looking after John.'

The two women hugged, both promising to keep in touch, and Eva waved Sal off. Her sister would have her work cut out, but with a husband and loving parents, Eva knew that she would be alright. She wished that Nikki's problem could be solved as easily. She returned to the office to clear up a few things that she had neglected to do earlier. She felt a mixture of satisfaction; at least her sister was happy. Thinking now of David and what had happened to him, she felt unsettled. She finished writing her report and put it on Beattie's desk; Eva wanted her to look up the section of the law she was interested in. She left the office, and made her way home. It was getting dark now as she drove along, hoping that Brian had finished his business for the day. He was waiting for her, a smile on his face as he kissed her.

'I have managed to book a table at that new restaurant, darling. Put your glad rags on, we'll have a relaxing evening for once. We can forget for a while everything that's been happening, and I know that we could both do with a break.' Eva was delighted and quickly showered. She chose a black shift dress to wear which complimented her fair hair; this she put up in a chignon. Brian whistled appreciatively.

'Wow, now I feel underdressed.'

'You'll do,' she laughed, noting his grey sports jacket. He seldom wore a tie, thinking them stuffy. To her mind, although not handsome in the conventional way, he had a nice face, one that you immediately trusted. She liked the way he raised one eyebrow whenever he needed an answer, making his face a little lopsided. She knew that a lot of her friends regarded him as attractive.

On the way to the restaurant, she told him about her meeting with Sal and the fact that she was going to have a baby. As Eva thought about it now, she realised that Brian had never discussed children, or that he would have liked to have had kids, consequently the subject had never come up. He knew of course about the miscarriage that she had had, and had been sympathetic about the anguish that she had gone through. She sighed, straightened her shoulders. It was time to look to the future.

The restaurant was obviously a popular one, judging by the amount of people who had chosen to eat there, Eva thought, as they entered. It was a large building with the restaurant on the ground floor. The upper floor looked like converted flats or some kind of business. She had spotted a few well-dressed people in evening dress going up the carpeted stairs. Could it be a gambling casino? She would ask Brian sometime whether he knew what was going on upstairs.

Eva had not been to this particular restaurant before. She could see, however, what would draw diners to it. The decor itself was subdued and tasteful. The tables all had flowers with candles gently flickering on them, giving an overall impression of delicate ambience. Soft music played while they waited for their food which, although not up to the standard of the Empress hotel which was second to none, was good. She marvelled at the way the chef had wrapped the asparagus in lemon grass, which was served on a bed of artichoke leaves and rice. Eva noticed that a number of the customers smiled at them, a few even coming across to where they were sitting to say hello.

'Friendly around here, aren't they?' she remarked. Brian nodded but said nothing. They were seated in an alcove; Eva looking around the crowded room thought that they had been lucky to get such a secluded table.

Brian filled her glass; her mind flashed back to when she and David had listened to the professor's lecture. She had been offered the same Chardonnay; someone had good taste she had thought at the time. She raised the glass to her lips, but she couldn't suppress a shudder; it all seemed like a bad dream. She missed David and his great charm.

She hadn't realised what a big part of her life he had been. They had been friends a long time, even before she had been called to the bar. The trust and companionship they had shared was rare and one that she would miss. He had told her once that he would always watch out for her. She knew that he would have gone out of his way to help her if she needed him… now he was gone. She wondered what the latest in the investigation was; she had forgotten to phone Marsh. That would have to wait until tomorrow now.

The music was soft and intimate; a few couples were dancing on the tiny dance floor, their bodies swaying to the music. She watched them for a moment, remembering another time, another age. Brian reached across and put his hand over hers.

'Enjoying yourself, darling?' Eva realised that she was. They didn't go out as much as she would have liked; between her schedule and Brian's long hours, the opportunity never seemed to arise very often. The coffee afterwards was excellent. She guiltily poured extra cream onto hers. He smiled across at her; her face was flushed, her eyes bright. He had never seen her looking so radiant. They stayed for a while, enjoying the peace they both felt.

'Ready?' he asked when he saw that she had started collecting her coat. She nodded, feeling relaxed and contented. Brian raised his hand to the head waiter. 'Bill please,' he said as he withdrew notes from his wallet. The waiter shook his head and smiled.

'Mr Reynolds, put your money away, sir. Mr Sard sends his compliments, and has instructed us to offer you our services at any time that you frequent his premises. We haven't seen so much of you lately. Mr Sard will be glad to know you are still around.' Eva saw the look of annoyance on Brian's face.

'I wasn't aware that Mr Sard owned this restaurant. Give my regards to him, and thank him for his generosity, but I prefer to pay my way,' indicating the wad of notes he had left on the plate. The waiter nodded.

'I quite understand, sir,' he said as he pushed back Eva's chair. Eva had to hurry to catch up with Brian as she followed him out into the street, and turned to face him. 'What was that about?' she asked, aware that he still had a frown of annoyance on his face. He saw her worried look and smiled. She could see, however, that it was an effort for him.

'Don't worry your little head over it, darling, I will sort it out.'

Eva's face flamed. She was incensed at his patronising tone, which was so unlike him. He knew how hard she had worked struggling against a mostly male environment; he knew also that she hated people talking down to anyone like that. Angrily she started to walk away, but he caught up with her, his face full of contrition.

'God, Eva, I am so sorry, it came out all wrong. I just meant that I would sort it out. Have I spoilt our evening by my stupidity?' He looked so crestfallen, she found herself laughing out loud at the expression on his face.

'Oh, let's forget it. You can make it up to me when we get home,' adding when she saw his face, 'I mean a nice massage, my neck is aching so much,' she told him grinning. It was a lovely evening, the night mild for late summer. They decided to stroll a while, enjoying just being together.

With a start, Eva realised that they were passing the very park where she had spent that awful night. She shuddered as she remembered. It was also near to where David had lost his life. Brian seemed unaware of what was going through her head as, with his arm around her, he kissed her.

'When are you going to make an honest man of me?' He was grinning, but became serious. 'Why, Eva, we love each other. I want us to marry. What is it that is stopping you? I'm not Stephen, you know.'

'I know you are not, give me a little more time,' she pleaded. He shook his head, but said nothing. She could tell though that he was hurt at her answer. When they reached home Eva was thoughtful. 'Brian, tell me what that little scene with the waiter was all about.'

'Oh you mean when he wanted to pay for our dinner? Yes, that was unfortunate. I wasn't aware that Akeem Sard owned that restaurant as well as the gambling establishment upstairs.'

'I wondered where all those people were going.' Her face cleared. 'But who is he?' she asked.

'He, my love,' he told her, 'was our main competitor, or he is working for the people who were. It is he, on their behalf, that put in a planning application for the luxury flats to be built where I want the centre, acting for a very large company who buy up and build luxury places for the wealthiest of people.'

'There must be important people behind the project and very rich ones too. With such powerful people, how could you have hoped to win with so much money behind it?' Eva was puzzled, wondering why she hadn't questioned Brian more on the procedures regarding the planning process.

'That's what makes our democracy so great. We were on a level playing field where planning applications are involved. We both have lawyers to put our case before the council. We stood as much chance as the next person,' he said smiling at her.

Eva had another thought. 'Brian, David's sister mentioned something at his funeral which worried me. It was about the planning application. There had been a suggestion that David might have swayed the vote your way because of our friendship. I know that I have mentioned it before.' Eva shivered. 'I couldn't take it on board then because of the circumstances of his death, but now... do you think that there would be any truth in it?' She was watching him, and for a moment she saw an expression she didn't understand cross his face. What was it? Whatever it was, it was gone so fast she thought that she may have been mistaken, because he smiled as he reassured her.

'Oh, Eva, we all know David would have done anything for you... anything,' he repeated in a strange voice, 'but not that. He was completely on the side of what was right. To interfere with any vote would not have entered his head, he took his job very seriously, as you know. Forget about it.' That conversation stayed with Eva, as later events made her recall it.

17.

Sam Holland answered the door himself, when the two policemen called. Marsh had Lenny with him. He wanted to give the young detective some experience of interviewing. Marsh knew the younger officer still had a lot to learn, but he thought that this was a start. It was pleasant out so the two detectives had walked the short distance to Lime Street. Marsh had waited until the evening; there was a good chance that both men would be in at that time.

'Good evening, Mr Holland.' Marsh identified himself and continued, 'I am in charge of the investigation into the death of Councillor David Sharpe. This is Detective Myers,' nodding his head towards Lenny. 'I believe you were present at the lecture given by Professor Shaw?'

'That's correct, Inspector, I was with my girlfriend. She actually got the tickets. What's this about?' His gaze shifted from Marsh to Lenny. Not unfriendly, Marsh thought, but watchful. He was a well-built young man. The detective noticed he wore designer jeans, Adidas trainers and an air of confidence that only the young can get away with. Lenny had his notebook out and was busy taking notes in it.

'We just want to confirm what you told my officers when questioned after the incident,' Marsh said. 'In the statement that you gave then, you said that you did not see anything unusual in the hall or afterwards, is that correct?' The man nodded.

'I believe, sir, that you have been in trouble with the police in the past.' Marsh saw that the man now had an angry look on his face.

'Don't you people ever give up? I was nineteen at the time, running wild with some other dudes, that's all in the past. Haven't you got better things to do than dig up incidents that happened long ago?'

'Yes, we do seem to dredge up old histories, but occasionally it pays off.' Marsh smiled at the man. He sympathised. He himself had had a run in with the local Bobby when he was young. That experience changed his life, however; the officer in question took him under his wing and it was at that time that he had become interested in police work. However, he had to forget about his personal feelings, he had a job to do.

'How well did you know Councillor Sharpe?' he asked, changing tactics.

'You mean the guy who was killed? I didn't know him, knew nothing about him until your two officers questioned me about him.'

Peter believed the man was telling the truth; he seemed a straight talker. Pike had found no connection with Sharpe. He had a good job, which he had held down for five years now. Thanking him, the two officers walked back to headquarters to pick up the file on Adil Flint. The inspector wondered if the next witness would prove a waste of time too. On the other hand, it was useful to put witnesses like Holland at the back of the list, and if nothing else turned up, to rethink his evidence.

Cambridge Gardens was a cul-de-sac off the main road; it had neat little houses and well-kept gardens. Marsh had decided to round off the day by questioning both of the witnesses that Pike had shortlisted, on the same day, while his mind was fresh. The two detectives made their way up the path. Just as they reached the door, however, it flew open. A large red-faced man stood there. He was much taller than either of the two officers, and Marsh hoped that there was not going to be any rough stuff. He felt, rather than saw, Lenny stiffen beside him. The big man was clearly angry. He wore a tight-fitting Hugo Boss lounge suit, and what Marsh always thought of as American loafers. He was obviously on his way out.

'If you are selling anything, I am not interested.'

To Marsh's ears the Bosnian still had a slight accent, although he must have been very young when he had arrived in this country. The detective judged him to be about forty. He thought it likely that the big man staring angrily at them now could, if need be, look after himself.

'We're sorry to have to bother you, Mr Flint. We are investigating the death of a man who was at a lecture given by Professor Shaw, on 10 September. I believe, sir, that you were also there. We just need to verify a couple of points. Do you mind if we come in?'

Marsh had no idea why he had asked that. Something in the man's eyes, a wary look perhaps, made the detective want to know more about him. The man seemed about to refuse then ungraciously led the way into a spacious front room.

'I was just on my way out, so make it snappy.' They were not invited to sit, but Marsh did so anyway, indicating to Lenny to do the same. Although he understood the man's frustration, the sooner he was eliminated from their enquiries, the sooner they could get on with their job of finding the killer of David Sharpe. Lenny had taken out his notebook and had started to write in it.

'Mr Flint…' Marsh began then paused. 'That's not the name you came into this country with, I believe?'

'You have been doing your homework. No, I was called Kresnik Berisha.' Flint shrugged. 'With a name like that, I found it hard to get employment, I changed it, anything wrong with that?' The man had a defiant look on his face as though challenging the inspector to find fault. Marsh ignored the jibe and said instead, 'How well did you know Councillor David Sharpe?'

Flint's eyes seemed to flicker. He asked quickly, 'Who?' He sounded puzzled, but Marsh thought that he had seen the same wary look as before pass over his face at the mention of Sharpe's name; he knew the man's expression could mean anything. He had had a run in with the authorities when he was younger; could be that memory had left a bad taste in his mouth.

'He is the man that was killed the night of the lecture. You must have heard about it. When did you leave the building?' As Marsh spoke, he looked around the surprisingly well-kept room. It was not a room he would have associated with a single fellow. Expensive rugs covered the floor, a picture hung on the wall which looked like an original Huxley, a bowl of fresh flowers stood on the polished table.

'I came out with the others, I didn't see anything. I heard later that some guy had been run over, but I had left by then.' The man seemed to relax.

'Were you with anyone at the talk, Mr Flint?' Marsh asked.

'No, I went alone, why you asking? If you want to know how I got the ticket, it was through the normal channels. I had booked it when I had heard who was giving the lecture.' The defiant look had returned to Flint's face.

'We are just checking the facts that we have. I have one more question, sir. What made you want to go to the lecture? Are you interested in Professor Shaw's book?' It was a loaded question and one Marsh disliked using. However, Flint didn't seem put out by it.

'Yeah, well I thought that it would be interesting. I read a lot and I knew his work, okay?'

'Well, thank you for all your help, sir.' The inspector got to his feet, Lenny rising at the same time. 'We will be in touch, if we need to speak to you again.' As they went along the path they could still see Flint standing staring after them. 'Well, laddie, how do you think that went?' Marsh glanced at his companion anxious to see if Lenny had picked up what he had.

'He looked a bit put out when you mentioned Mr Sharpe's name. I noticed, boss, that you didn't mention his previous record.' Lenny kept up with the older detective's long strides as they walked along the darkened street.

'Yes, I didn't want to spook him. A very interesting man, he had a very expensive Rolex on, and did you notice that painting, and the clothes that he was wearing? They are what we old folks would describe as snazzy, which means you wouldn't get them at M&S. I want you to run a check on his finances, check with the VAT chaps and credit companies. I would like to know more about our Mr Krasnik Berisha alias Adil Flint.'

Feeling as though the evening had not been entirely wasted, Marsh left Lenny to check up on Flint, and went along to the superintendent's office to bring him up to date with what had been happening. He had been in touch regularly with the Scotland Yard officers, and to the inspector's relief they had not interfered in any way since their last encounter. He knew that it was early days yet, and more checking to be done, but he was satisfied with the way it was going – only hoped his boss was too. As he entered his office, his superintendent looked up.

'Ah, Peter, I was just heading up to see you, you've saved me the exercise,' which, Marsh thought wryly, his boss was in serious need of; his belt had long ago disappeared under a roll of fat. He filled him in on the latest developments, telling him his feelings regarding Flint.

'I think that we may have something here. I would be very interested to know where all his money comes from,' he said, adding, 'I've sent young Lenny to do some more checking. I am hoping that he may find something that might help us. What did you want to see me about?' he asked as he saw that his boss was holding a piece of paper in his hand.

'I have just been speaking to Superintendent Miles from the uniform branch. He told me that on the night Councillor Sharpe was killed, the switchboard had a call reporting a man acting drunk and disorderly near the hall where the lecture was taken place, even gave his name: Mr David Sharpe.'

'That doesn't make any sense, did the caller leave a name?' Marsh drew in a deep breath as his boss shook his head.

'To confuse us even more, the call was timed at 8pm.' He turned to Marsh. 'What time did the lecture finish?' he asked. 'It broke up early due to the professor feeling unwell,' Marsh told him, and continued, 'The post-mortem states the time of death before 8pm. I have heard of dead man walking, but this is ridiculous. Mr Sharpe was dead before the call was made.' What was this all about? Marsh was confused. Who had phoned the police to complain about a man who was probably dead by that time? Marsh stopped, his mind racing. What if the people who gave Mr Sharpe the drug had not meant to kill him, but… what? Perhaps to discredit him? Who would want to do that and why? Marsh was aware that events were moving fast now.

18.

Brian was even busier than usual, now that the go ahead for the centre had been given. He was determined not to waste any more time. It was important for him to get the funding back on track. Eva knew that he was chasing up all his contacts who had promised donations once the planning application had been accepted, and she was happy for him. However, she seldom saw him to have a conversation with anymore. When he was home, he was in his study. He had been out all day. He had phoned her briefly to tell her not to wait up. She didn't mind, but she missed the times that they had shared. She was glad, however, that at last his hard work was coming to fruition. She rang Nikki, aware that she had not been in touch lately. Her friend's voice sounded bright over the phone; Eva was surprised. The last time they had spoken, Nikki had been unhappy and talking about splitting with Nigel.

'What's been happening?' she asked her friend.'Eva, I meant to phone you before now, but something always seemed to come up.' Nikki's voice was breathless. 'We have got back together again, Nigel and me, I mean. Isn't it wonderful?'

Eva agreed, thinking things seemed to be good everywhere at the moment. The friends made a date to meet up and Eva put the phone down as she heard the front door opening. She frowned; Brian had said that he would be late tonight. She glanced at the clock; only seven. He must have finished earlier than he had thought. She waited for him to join her in the front room; instead she heard the study door close and then silence. Puzzled she went towards the study; she could hear him on the phone. His voice sounded different: low and urgent. When he saw her at the door, he quickly replaced the receiver and stared at her. She was really concerned now; although he seemed to be looking at her, it was as though he didn't see her. She ran to him.

'Darling, what's wrong?' She could see now that his face was white; the hand that reached out to her was shaking.

'Eva,' was all he said as he buried his head in his hands. She quickly poured out a stiff whiskey for him. He had obviously had some kind of shock. She felt that the drink would revive him. He took the glass from her and with hands that were shaking drained it. It was the second time he had done that in just a few days. He seemed to pull himself together and gave her a thin smile, which did nothing to console her.

'What is it, Brian?'

'Eva, I have had to withdraw the plans for the centre.' His voice was hoarse as though he had a cold. She stared at him unable or unwilling to believe what she had heard.

'What do you mean?'

'Can't you understand? There isn't going to be a centre now.' His voice suddenly rose as he stared angrily at her. He stood up. 'Now if you'll excuse me I have a lot of calls to make, I haven't got time for this.' Eva stared uncomprehendingly at him, as he almost pushed her out of the room. She couldn't believe that he had spoken to her like that, had dismissed her as though she was a child. What was happening? Stunned, she stood outside the door which he had abruptly closed behind her, her mind in turmoil. She wanted to fling the door open and confront him. However, she had seen something in his eyes that she had never seen before: the look of a stranger. She made her way back to the front room trying to think what she ought to do.

Brian had deliberately kept her away from any of his associates; he had told her once when she had queried the fact that she didn't know who his colleagues were that he didn't want her bothered by them ringing up at their home and it had never happened. Consequently there was no one she could call now to clarify what was happening. She had no names, and no one whom she could contact. She wondered why she hadn't thought it strange before now that none of his colleagues had ever been invited to the house for a meal or even a drink. Despite Brian's explanation she had thought it unusual.

She had to speak to someone whom she could trust. Her mind went to David; although he had said some outrageous things, she had trusted him, he would have advised her. Eva missed him so much. She didn't have him to advise her, but she had Ted. Her stepfather had been a successful barrister before he had retired; his integrity was beyond question. She lifted the phone, hoping that Ted was there; it was a relief when she heard his voice.

'Eva, what a pleasant surprise to hear from you. Do you want to speak to your mother?' His voice was wonderfully normal.

'Hi Ted.' She paused wondering how to go on. He made

it easy for her; he must have heard something in her voice.

'What is it, Eva, is Brian alright?'

'What have you heard?' She was alarmed; Ted had always kept his ear to the ground, often surprising her with information even she hadn't known.

'I have heard nothing, what's happened?' His voice was quieter now; Eva guessed that her mother was near.

'I wondered, Ted, whether we could meet somewhere. I need your advice, Dad.' Ted's voice was thick with emotion when he spoke.

'Thank you, darling, for that. You know I will meet you wherever you want.'

They arranged to meet midway between their two homes. Eva was careful to choose a place away from where her mother might venture on one of her coffee sprees. Eva wasn't ready yet to say anything to her until she knew herself what it was all about. Ted entered the pub-cum-restaurant a few minutes after Eva had arrived. He saw her sitting in a booth, her head bowed. He sat down opposite, giving her hand a squeeze as he did so, his eyes concerned. She smiled shakily up at him.

'Thanks so much for coming, Dad.' She was glad that she had addressed him like that, as she saw his eyes light up. Eva chided herself for not doing so before this. Although not her biological father, Ted had done more to help her than her real dad had. He had seen her through the aftermath of the breakup of her marriage, the loss of her baby, and helped her on the road to her career.

They ordered coffee. Ted sat sipping his coffee as he watched her, seeing again something of the young confused Eva she had been all those years ago. Sitting opposite, he was concerned. What could have happened to cause Eva to look… he searched for the word… so desperate looking? She suddenly starting talking, telling him everything that had occurred when she had found herself on the bench in the park. Ignoring the incredulity on Ted's face, she continued talking, putting her hand up when he tried to intervene.

'Please let me finish, Dad, otherwise I might not be able to, as it gets worse.' He nodded, and she told him about the photograph which had been taken of her on that park bench. She saw that her stepfather's expression had changed to one of horror. She came to the part that was the latest development: Brian telling her that he was withdrawing his planning application. She also told him about his strange mood. 'I have no clue whose Brian's contacts are. I wondered if you could talk to him.' She knew that Brian got on well with Ted; maybe he might tell him what was going on; she hoped so. Ted immediately assured her that he would do everything in his power to help her.

'It should be an easy job to find out who is on the board of the charity, but I will hold fire until I have spoken to Brian. It might not be as bad as you imagine.' Giving her a hug, and telling her again that he would do his best to help her, Ted watched Eva drive away, a worried frown on his face. Earlier he had heard some unsettling news about Brian, although he had not mentioned it to Eva; she had enough to worry about with this latest development. He wondered if what he had heard about him was true. It was rumoured that Brian had been seen at the gambling tables. He seemed to have his head screwed on where business was concerned. Perhaps the stories of him being seen at a casino were exaggerated; he hoped so.

Driving home, Eva felt as though a load had been lifted off her shoulders. She was glad that she had told Ted. She knew that what she had said would go no further. She arrived home to an empty house, and for one awful moment Eva was afraid that Brian had gone; she was relieved when she saw his clothes still in the wardrobe. She had turned her mobile off through force of habit, but she saw that Brian had left a message to tell her that he would be home later.

19.

Inspector Marsh sent a car to pick up Adil Flint. This was unusual but he had been to a meeting, which had taken longer than first thought. He would have liked to have gone to talk to Flint at his home. Suspects – the detective now believed Flint to be in that category – relaxed more when interviewed at home. However, he was anxious to speak to the man again.

He knew that Flint will probably kick up a fuss. He was prepared for this and had instructed whoever was going to pick him up to do so with some tact, knowing that Flint was under no obligation to co-operate with the police. Coleen Daley, however, had described the man whom she had seen half-carrying a woman across the road as tall with light-coloured long hair. Although she was not exactly sure of her facts, Marsh thought that it was worth interviewing Flint again to see his reactions when faced with a witness who described the man she saw as looking like him.

With Flint picked up – and according to the officer detailed to do that, it had been with bad grace, refusing at first to accompany the police, but eventually agreeing to do so – now Marsh studied the man through the window of the interview room. The inspector had to admit he now seem unconcerned. He nodded to Pike to join him and together they entered the room. Flint glanced up and gave an appreciative grin when he saw Pike enter.

'Nice,' he said even making the word sound offensive.

Marsh turned on the recording machine. 'This is an interview with Adil Flint also known as Kresnik Berisha. For the remainder of this interview he shall be known as Adil Flint. With him are Detective Inspector Peter Marsh and Detective Constable Sandra Pike. Mr Flint, I am obliged to tell you that you are not under arrest, and can leave at any time you choose. Do you understand, sir?'

'Yeah.'

'You agree to answer questions put to you by myself or Detective Pike?'

'Get it over with, why don't you.'

Marsh saw that Flint was getting impatient. The man could walk at any time, which he didn't want. To relax him Marsh offered him a cup of tea which he declined.

'I won't keep you long, sir, I just want to clarify a couple of points. You said in your statement that you didn't know Councillor Sharpe. Is that correct?'

'That's right.' Flint's voice was surly now.

'You also stated that you did not see Ms Eva Sinclair at the lecture or know who she was?'

'Yes,' he said warily now.

'Would it surprise you to learn that an eyewitness has told us that they saw a man fitting your description crossing the road with Ms Sinclair?'

'That's a lie, I never even knew the woman.' Flint's voice was full of anger. Suddenly he grinned. 'I see what your little game is, Inspector, you accuse, then settle back and wait for some poor blighter to fall down at your feet confessing all.'

'I don't see you falling down confessing all, Mr Flint.' Marsh was amused. There was an element of truth in what the man had said.

'That's because I have nothing to confess.' Flint got to his feet, yawning. 'Next time you want to talk to me, Inspector, I will have a lawyer with me.' With a lewd wink at Pike, he asked, 'Am I free to go now?'

Marsh got to his feet also and held out his hand; although he was disappointed with the interview, he admired the way the man handled himself. The policeman had not got what he was after, but he had Flint on record saying that he had not known the judge; that might be useful later on. He certainly was a cool customer, Marsh thought. He had known innocent people go to pieces once they were questioned. Psychoanalysts have told him that all of us have some guilty secret, whether small or large. We feel that our small indiscretions might be revealed when questioned by authority. He signalled to a uniformed officer to see Flint out, and then turned to Pike and raised an eyebrow.

'Well, how do you think that went?'

'I have a strong stomach, sir,' she gave a little shiver, 'but I would not like to meet Mr Adil Flint alone without a Taser handy.'

Marsh smiled at her. 'Unfortunately we can't arrest a person because we don't like the look of them.' He returned to the interview room and removed the recording of the interview from the machine. He knew the police now had highly technical equipment to interview people, but Marsh liked to stick to what he understood, and this interview, as short as it had been, may come in useful if needed later.

He and Pike made their way upstairs. He was anxious

to hear how Lenny had got on checking out the Flint's finances. He found the sergeant pinning up photographs of the people that had been interviewed. Lenny was in the corner writing in his notebook; Marsh could see that the page was filled with neat writing. He was quickly changing his opinion of Lenny; after his initial complaining, he had done the jobs he had been asked to do. Marsh was keen to see what he had discovered about Flint's lifestyle.

'It's all in there, sir,' he told Marsh handing him the file. Briefly he outlined what he had found out. 'Mr Flint runs a small haulage business, which seems to be doing alright. He has two men working for him. The one that I spoke to was noncommittal regarding his boss. I suspected, from what he didn't say, that he was not too popular with the people who worked for him.'

'Did the VAT people get back to you?'

'Yes, sir! His books balance,' he said handing the inspector another piece of paper.

'So all this adds up to what?' Marsh asked glancing down at the figures on the sheet Lenny had given to him. 'To the fact that we have no way of knowing where the money for the items like the Rolex watch comes from. Not his business, where, according to this,' he said holding up the sheet from the VAT people, 'the work is steady, but certainly not doing well enough for those little extras. It is a pity that I didn't have these figures earlier before I let Flint go. Ah well, it looks like another visit to Mr Flint. Who wants to come with me?' he laughed looking at Pike.

'I will come with you, sir,' she told him grinning.

20.

Eva's stepfather waited outside the flat she shared with Brian. He saw the man he was looking out for walking slowly along the road. Ted had parked his car near to their home so that he would be able to speak to Brian before he went inside. He wasn't sure that had he knocked, Brian would have opened the door.

'Hi Brian, got time for a cup of coffee?' he called, climbing out of his car. He noticed that Eva's partner looked pale. He walked along as though all the strength had been drained out of him. Where, Ted wondered, was that vigorous man he had seen just a week or so ago, the man who had treated them all to a celebratory dinner? Brian raised a hand in greeting, but carried on walking. Ted was puzzled, had the man not heard him? He hurried after him. 'Brian, wait.' This time he stopped and faced the older man.

'Did Eva put you up to this?' There was accusation as well as anger in his voice.

'She is really worried about you, Brian. Can't we go somewhere quiet and discuss it? I am a good listener. Eva tells me that you haven't spoken to her about the reason you decided to pull out of the project.'

'I haven't been able to.' Then as though resigned to it, he said, 'Let's go in, Eva won't be home for a while yet.' He led the way into the flat and into the front room. The sun was shining through the French windows and Brian, with a hint of his old self said, 'Eva will kill me. She asked me to pull the blinds down, the sun fades the carpets. I forgot this morning, had rather a lot on my mind.'

'I won't tell her.' Ted smiled, glad to see that Brian hadn't lost all his sense of humour. Later, sitting nursing the worst coffee Ted had ever tasted, he raised the subject again. 'Tell me why, Brian. You have worked so hard for the centre. Why have you withdrawn the plans?'

'It wasn't such a good bet as we had thought.' Brian shrugged. 'The overheads would have been enormous. We got it wrong, as simple as that.'

'I don't buy that,' Ted told him shaking his head. 'I was in the position of looking over the costing, don't ask me how, anyway they were spot on. What was the real reason?' They stared at one another, both determined men, then Brian's shoulders slumped.

'Okay, Ted, but you must promise to keep to yourself what I am about to tell you.'

'As long as it doesn't involve Eva getting hurt, then yes,' Ted nodded his assent, 'I will keep it to myself.

'That's quite ironic, because it does concern Eva.' When Ted started to remonstrate, Brian held up his hand.

'You wanted to know, so please let me finish. Did Eva ever tell you about the night she wound up on a park bench?' As the older man nodded, Brian continued, 'Someone took a photo of her while she was lying on that damned bench. 'It's pretty awful, anyway they, whoever they are, threatened to put it all over the web if I didn't withdraw the planning application. I couldn't allow her to be shown like that. So I did what they told me.'

Ted was horrified by what he had heard. It was a big sacrifice Brian had made, but it surely couldn't end there. What about the board that Brian was answerable to? They would not be interested in his private life, but they would be interested to know why the application had been withdrawn. However, he was grateful to Brian and said so.

'Thank you, son, I admire what you have done, and I know that you did this because you love Eva, but be sensible, lad. You have to let the police know that there are people out there who are doing this kind of thing, they need to be stopped.'

'Yes I am sure that we could find them.' Brian shrugged helplessly. 'But at what cost to Eva? We have our hands tied at the moment…' He broke off when he saw Eva at the door.

'Whose hands are tied?' she asked coming into the room looking questioningly at the two men. They both went towards her. Ted was the first to get over his surprise at seeing her.

'My hands are tied to your mother's apron. She will be wondering where I have got to. I must be on my way.' He felt a bit mean leaving Brian to explain the unexplainable. He needed to think about what Brian had just told him. He knew that there were people out there who were capable of doing such things, indeed he had met a few when he was a barrister, but now it was personal. He gave Eva a hug murmuring so that Brian couldn't hear.

'Everything is going to be alright, Eva. Trust Brian, he is a good man.' She looked searchingly at him, then she smiled, the relief she felt showing on her face as she hugged him. Ted knew he had said the right thing. 'I will ring you,' he told her as she saw him out. For the first time since the day of the exchange with Brian, Eva felt that perhaps things were not as black as first thought. Brian didn't say much to her, but he was attentive, preparing the meal they had and later as they sat quietly looking at one another he said, 'I am so sorry, Eva.' He took her hand, his face full of remorse. 'My actions were unpardonable, please forgive me.' She nodded, unable to speak as he went on. 'I have told Ted about my decision. He agrees that for the moment it's the right one. He has given me his word that he would not tell you, please don't ask him.'

Eva was confused. What had she got to do with the decision that Brian had made? Perhaps he was concerned that it would take up more of his time; that he would be away from her more often. She strove to convince him that she was behind him all the way, not minding if it kept them apart more often. Brian smiled, a far away expression on his face as though he hadn't heard her.

That evening Eva felt that it had all been a bad dream. Their relationship had taken a knocking but sitting close together as they now were, Brian's arm around her, she felt it was all in the past; their lives would get back to the way they were. She couldn't, however, forget how Brian had acted. He had been like a stranger, not the loving man who wanted to marry her. She shivered as she remembered the way he had closed the door on her; it had felt like he had been shutting her out of his life.

'You're trembling, my love, are you cold?' He pulled her closer, concern on his face.

'Just a bit tired. It was a busy day today.' Eva smiled up at him, wishing with all her heart that she could forget the feeling that his treatment of her had left. What about the plans for the centre now, were they going to be shelved? She wanted to question Brian, but for the first time since they had met, she was unsure of the reaction she might get.

'Is Beattie giving you too many cases? I will have to have a word with her.'

For a while now, Brian and Beattie had made an unspoken pact between them to shield Eva whenever possible. But she failed to understand what they were shielding her from. And at first she had been amused, but lately their attention had grated.

'I wish you and Beattie would find some other interest, it's becoming distracting knowing you two are discussing what I am or am not doing.'

'You should be grateful, darling, that you are loved by so many people who only want the best for you.' Brian's reproachful look made Eva feel that she was indeed being ungrateful; surely she should be glad to be cared for that way, but she wasn't. It had been a long time since she had to rely on anyone but herself. She was too old now too start.

'I am sorry, but I can look after myself quite well.' *Can I though? I haven't made such a good job of it lately*, she thought as Brian remained silent.

21.

Marsh knew that they would get another frosty reception from Flint; this was the third time the police had spoken to him, but he was unprepared for the way the man threw open his door shouting, 'Unless you are here to arrest me, you can fuck off.' Although the policeman was taken aback, he was also amused. The man had balls, no doubt about it, he thought admiringly. He was ready to go up against the power of British law and all it involved.

'Yes I know that we are a damned nuisance,' he said quietly, 'but my boss will hang me out to dry if I go back without talking to you.'

Pike, listening to her boss almost pleading with a prime suspect, felt embarrassed, then she saw a grin appear on Flint's face.

'You crafty so and so, come on in then,' he said with a wink at Pike. Marsh followed the man into the house. She fingered her Taser, convinced that it would be needed soon.

'That's better,' Marsh said sitting down and taking out his notebook. 'Now where were we? Ah yes, you must have known that we would look into your finances, Mr Flint. Apparently your books are all in order.' He saw a satisfied grin appear on the man's face, as he continued, 'The question remains, however: where did the money come from to buy that watch you have on? I can also see around this room, there are some nice pieces. Those rugs for instance must have set you back a fair sum.'

'Nice, aren't they?' Flint's grin didn't go. 'Alright, Inspector, I will stop playing games with you. I gamble… See! I knew that you wouldn't believe me,' he exclaimed seeing Marsh's look of scepticism.

'I know,' Marsh told him, 'but you must admit that it is the standard answer we get whenever we ask where extra money comes from.' Flint went over to the dresser and took a card from it and handed it to the inspector.

'My membership card to the casino. Go on have a shifty, it's all in order.'

Marsh took the card. The address was in the centre of town. Marsh knew the establishment well; he knew quite a lot of well-connected people went there. What surprised the policeman was that they would allow a man like Flint to become a member. He didn't want to be an elitist, but it was very exclusive, used by the wealthiest in town. He was not sure whether he himself would be welcome. It was worth checking out to see if what Flint had said was true. Marsh stood up; he shook Flint's hand. He liked the man's spirit, and it seemed to be mutual as Flint told him, 'If there's anything you need to move, Inspector, furniture and the like, I'm your man. I will give you a good rate too.'

As they drove away, Pike chanced a cheeky remark. 'Very chummy, sir.' She grinned, thinking that the more she saw of her boss and the way he dealt with awkward people, the more she admired him. He had brought a near dangerous situation to a satisfactory conclusion, getting what he wanted in the meantime. *Clever bugger*, she thought.

Marsh called his team together to summarise what they had got… 'We now know that Judge Sinclair had the same barbiturate in her bloodstream as Councillor David Sharpe. She has stated that she drank some of his orange juice. We are certain that the drug was in that drink.'

'We questioned everyone,' Pike looked up from her notes, 'including the organisers. They saw no one in particular near the drinks. Oh, they all said that plenty of people were milling around, but no one stood out. There was only one waiter. Lenny and I have scrutinised his record… Nothing, and no reasons have emerged to make us suspicious of him.'

'The only suspect, and that's just a gut feeling, is Adil Flint. Did you check on his membership, and whether he has been lucky at the tables, Sergeant?' Marsh asked.

'I sure did, I went further,' Roger replied, 'I made an application to become a member myself, just to see what would happen. Guess what? It was intimated by the snotty receptionist that I wouldn't be welcome there as a member.'

'Who would want a penury policeman like you sitting among the toffs?' Lenny laughed loudly at his colleague's answer.

'You are dead right, son, told me just that. However, the boss thinks a lot of our Mr Flint. According to the same doorman, he spends a lot of his time in the offices talking to the owner, who goes by the name of Sard. His record is above reproach, a nationalised Briton, supports local charities etc. Flint is a regular visitor and very lucky at the tables. Funny thing that, boss, the way the doorman said it, well… I didn't get the impression that he was that popular with the rest of the staff. The same as the men working at his haulage business, obviously not well liked anywhere.'

'As I said before, being unpopular doesn't mean you are a killer. On the other hand, I think if Flint is behind this, for reasons we have yet to discover, I don't believe he was acting alone.' Marsh told them about the 999 call, and what time it was called in. 'It couldn't have been Flint. If my suspicions are correct, he was busy escorting Judge Sinclair to the park and while there, I believe it was he who took the photograph of her.'

Marsh knew that he was going out on a limb here, which he knew was more up his superintendent's street, but he knew he was going to take a chance and go by what his instincts told him.

'I know it is all conjecture, but I think there might be enough here to get a search warrant soon. I would be very interested to see what is on his phone, and computer. We might even find out who he has been talking to and getting his instructions from.'

'That's a long shot, sir. In the meantime, what do you want us to do?' the sergeant asked.

'Well,' Marsh said slowly knowing he was going outside his remit, 'I have a feeling we are nearing a turning point here, but I would like to keep a daytime watch on Flint. We haven't enough officers to do a twenty-four-hour one. This is not an order, you can withdraw now if you wish, and we won't think any more of it.' He waited as his team eyed each other grinning, until Lenny, the clown of the team, spoke up.

'You're not leaving any of us out of this one, boss, but I'm not sitting in a car for any length of time with the sarge here. He grunts when he's dozing and when he is awake, he gets crisps an' crunches them ad nauseam.'

'If you buy that one, boss, then you are greener than I thought,' Roger said grinning. 'Can't you see where this is going? He wants to get all cosy with Pike.'

'Really, sir, I have no idea what the sarge here is talking about.' Pike's protest was loud. 'I have found that Detective Myers and I work well as a team, but I would work equally well with the sarge.' Marsh was amused but he hadn't the time to get involved.

'Pike, you and I do first watch, Sergeant, you and Lenny take second, and Roger, no crisps.' Marsh knew that he was taking a chance. The superintendent would, he knew, refuse his request for a search warrant at the moment. But he was hopeful that Flint might give him the excuse he needed to scrutinise his phone records. He had a strong feeling that Flint was their man, and if it could be proved that it was he who had given the drug to the councillor, his super might ignore what he was about to do.

'Right, Sergeant, you and Lenny get off home now, grab a bite to eat and have a rest. Pike and I will do first watch. I will phone you when we need to be relieved.'

Marsh and Pike got into the inspector's own car. It was one he rarely used for work, so no chance that Flint would recognise it. They drew up well away from the house that they were watching. As it was a cul-de-sac, Flint would have to go past. Marsh smiled; Pike and he could appear to be a couple if they were spotted. On the other hand, the inspector was keen to see who might visit the suspect, so he decided to park near a green space where they could keep an eye on their man through field glasses.

'We look like a couple of birdwatchers,' Pike said.

'That's the idea; we don't want the local Bobby turning

up because people have noticed us,' Marsh told her, making himself more comfortable in his seat, thinking it had been a long time since he had done a stake-out, as they call it in films. It was going to be a long day.

22

Eva had thought that now the planning application had been withdrawn, Brian would spend more time with her; the opposite had happened. She wondered where he went every day; if she hadn't known better, she might have thought that he was having an affair, apart from the fact that she knew that was out of the question. An affair would not leave him hollow-eyed, and tossing in his sleep at night, and looking wearier then he should have done. Eventually she phoned her stepfather, hoping that he might give her some idea what was going on. Ted sounded puzzled.

'Have you asked him what's bothering him, Eva?'

'Surely it must have something to do with the cancelling of the planning application and you know, Dad, he has never explained why he took that action anyway, but he told you the reason, didn't he?'

'As I understand it, Brian did what he had to do, and it should be at an end now.' Ted's voice held a worried note.

'Well, it's not, far from it. I don't know what to do,' she told her stepfather. 'I promised him that I wouldn't question the reasons behind his action, but I can't stand by and watch him looking so wretched. There is almost desperation in the way he looks.'

'In that case, Eva, you have to speak to him. You have to make it clear to him that you intend to find out what's going on. That should stir things up. Let me know how you get on.'

Eva thanked him and replaced the receiver thoughtfully. She didn't relish the thought of challenging Brian to tell her what was going on; she would never forget the look he had given her when he had almost shoved her out of the office door. She knew that it must be done. With a determined glance at the clock, Eva waited in the front room, leaving the door ajar in case she missed him. At last she heard Brian enter. Getting up from the chair that she had been sitting on, she ran to him putting her arms around him.

'Darling, let's go into the front room, I need to talk to you.' He shook his head trying to free himself from her grasp, but she held on. 'This is serious, Brian. I need you to tell me what's happening. If you don't trust me then I can't see any future with us.'

He stared at her, seemingly not taking in what she was saying, then his arms went around her and he buried his face in her hair. He seemed to be weighing up what he had to say to her. Then his arms dropped to his side as he went slowly into the front room, and turned to face her.

'You are right. God! Eva, the last thing I want is to lose you.' She followed him into the front room, and sat curled up at his feet, and listened as with a deep breath he said, 'I suppose that I should have told you about it in the first place. I didn't want you to think that you were responsible, darling, because you are not. They would have found some other way to get to me.'

'What are you talking about?' She stared at him bewildered. 'What am I not responsible for and who are they?'

'Let's start at the beginning.' Brian now seemed resigned as he told her. 'The photograph of you in the park, remember? Someone sent a copy of it to me. I was told that unless I withdrew the planning application, that photo would go viral on the internet, with the heading, "Would you trust your freedom with this judge?" Her gasp of horror made him tighten his arms around her. 'It's okay, love, I did what they asked me, you are safe now.'

'But at what cost to you and the people who were depending on the centre, Brian? Who are these people who can wreck lives?' She couldn't believe this was happening; Brian had sacrificed all that he believed in for her.

'I wish that I knew,' he sighed. 'The nightmare that I am still living with is that they may print it anyway.'

'Then why don't we inform the police?' Eva asked. 'They might find out who is behind it and you know, Brian, I think with all you have gone through for me, I wonder if it would be that bad. We would show the bastards that we are not to be intimidated.'

'That's a great sentiment,' he sighed again, 'but I don't think that it's the answer. Let's wait and see what happens now. It will be interesting to see how the council react with all the changes to the applications. It is not a straightforward procedure. Quite complicated in fact. I am surprised that they haven't asked more questions as it is. However, I feel a lot better since I told you. We will sort it out.' He put his arm around her; they were both deep in thought.

Eva felt overwhelmed with love for this man who had

done so much for her. She was tempted to get in touch with the inspector; she was sure that he would be angry that they had said nothing about the blackmail threat, allowing these people to get away with it. As a judge she knew that she could not stand by and do nothing. Suddenly she knew what she would do. She had decided. She would ring Marsh in the morning.

She couldn't allow the man she loved to give up on all that he and his board had worked for all these months. Again she wondered what Brian's board thought of it. How could he justify his actions to them? They must be businessmen and women, it didn't make any sense. She thought of these people who had driven them both into this corner. How she wished that they were before her in the dock. As she looked across at Brian, she noticed how crushed he seemed. *Well, that's got to stop.* She knew that sometimes online social media could be cruel in the extreme, but that was a risk she was prepared to take. She smiled at him, and straightened her shoulders. Her mind was made up.

23.

Marsh felt that the case was nearing closure. The staff sergeant had reported that Joe Quinn had been arrested and charged with the theft of a handbag. He had pleaded not guilty and, when asked, had declined a lawyer, which pleased Marsh. Although it is within the suspect's rights to have one present, sometimes it delays the proceedings from moving along.

Joe Quinn was well known to Marsh. He was a petty crook, who went after easy targets such as the elderly, and lifting anything that he could sell to feed his habit. He was an alcoholic, and could often be seen slouched in a doorway unconscious. He had spent many a night at Her Majesty's pleasure.

Now he sat bleary-eyed, squinting up at Marsh when he walked into the room. The inspector could see that he was emaciated, his ribs protruding through the thin top he had on. Pike was with the inspector, while the sergeant and Lenny were outside Flint's house. Marsh and Pike had spent a fruitless four hours watching the Bosnian, without any movement from the man. Pike had her notebook ready. Although the interview was being recorded, Marsh liked to have a visible script where he could scrutinise the interview later on.

'How are you, Joe?' Marsh asked. He looked at Pike. 'Ask the custody officer to bring in some food.' He asked, 'Chips okay?' Quinn nodded. 'Chips it is then, and some tea for all of us.' Pike was getting used to the way the detective worked when interviewing a suspect; winning their trust was a useful ploy, as in this case.

'Now, Joe,' Marsh said watching the man opposite cramming chips into his mouth, 'have you got anything to tell me off the record, before I put the tape on?' Joe Quinn stopped chewing, staring wide-eyed at the detective.

'What can I have to tell you, gov? I don't know what you mean.'

Marsh smiled grimly, this was the usual charade that was invariably played out by people who had something to hide. 'Cut the crap, Joe, but if that's the way you want to play it, have it your way,' he said nodding at Pike to turn the tape on. 'Inspector Peter Marsh, interviewing Joseph Quinn, 20 September at,' he looked at his watch, '3.30pm. With me is Detective Sandra Pike.' Addressing Quinn he asked, 'Can you confirm your name address and date of birth, sir.' The interview continued along the specified lines with the theft of the handbag and Joe Quinn's fingerprints on it, with Quinn answering just what he had to.

'Right, sir, that should do it. I will ask the custody officer to put you in one of the cells and…' Marsh was interrupted by Quinn who had at this time starting rubbing his hand across his mouth. Marsh knew the signs well; the man in front of him was getting desperate for alcohol.

"ere, what's going on? I have answered your bloody questions. I want to go home now.'

'Your rights have been read to you,' Marsh told him. 'You

are under arrest. I can hold you here until I get the answers that I want. The truth will do. We can prove that you took a handbag from the park bench... which did not belong to you. You know how it works, you give me something, and maybe I can return the favour.'

'Okay, what do you want to know?' Joe Quinn turned a defeated look at the inspector.

How easy it had been, Marsh thought feeling some relief. Sometimes the suspect would hang on until the last, hoping to get the best deal. The petty thief admitted that he had taken the bag. His voice had a whine to it, which was not lost on Marsh; he knew the man was longing for a drink.

'But it was on the floor, so I found it, right? I didn't know that it belonged to anyone, finders keepers.'

'If that's your story, Mr Quinn, though seeing that the owner was lying nearby, well... We will leave that for the present. I am interested in whether you saw the woman whom the bag belonged to arrive at the park bench, and who was with her?' 'What if I did? I still found the bag lying on the floor.'

'Forget about the bag for the moment.' Marsh was exasperated; this was going nowhere. He was impatient to find out what the other man knew. Pike stepped in.

'Did you know the bloke who dumped the lady on the bench, Mr Quinn?' she asked.

'Yeah, seen him around, ain't I.' His voice was sullen now.

'Where was that?' Marsh asked, sending Pike an approving look. Quinn rattled his tea cup and licked his lips. 'Thirsty work this.'

Marsh too was feeling the tension. It had been a long day and now that they were close to discovering the person who had carried Eva to the park, he wanted to shout at the man to stop messing them about; instead he sent Pike for more tea.

'Now, sir,' Marsh spoke through gritted teeth, 'can you identify the person you saw carrying the lady to the park?' Quinn stared at the detective.

'How many times do I have to say yes. Blimey, you people…' He didn't finish, as with a raised voice Marsh asked, 'What is his name, sir?'

'Flint or something, he owns a haulage business.'

'Yes!' Marsh almost said out loud, aware that the tape was recording the interview. All that remained was for Quinn to identify Flint as the man and Eva as the woman being carried by him. He saw that Pike was leaning forward now in her eagerness to make the most of what was happening. She knew that police work was ninety per cent hard graft, trying to get answers from people who didn't want to give them. This made up for the frustrations.

'The woman you saw, would you be able to recognise her again if I showed you a photograph?' He opened a file and took out a photograph of a serious-looking Eva. He held it out. 'Take your time, sir.' Marsh spoke formally now, aware that the tape might be used as evidence. Joe Quinn stared at the picture for a second, and grinned.

'Blimey, she looks a lot better here than she did when she was lying on the bench, blotto.'

'Sir, can you identify the woman in this photograph as the woman you saw on the park bench?'

'That's her alright. Can I go now?'

'The witness has identified the photograph as that of Ms Eva Sinclair.' Marsh was satisfied that the interview would stand up in court and Flint would be charged and found guilty of the abduction of the judge. Whether they could now secure evidence that he was also responsible for the death of David Sharpe was another matter.

Marsh left it to the custody officer to escort Quinn to the cells. He would let the man sweat in a cell overnight, and release him in the morning. Marsh felt that it would serve no purpose to take it any further. He felt drained but satisfied; his theory had proved correct. He phoned the sergeant who was keeping a watch on Flint.

'He hasn't moved, sir, but my backside is getting a bit sore.'

'Sergeant, take Lenny and arrest Flint on suspicion of abducting a person without their consent, and possibly a more serious charge to follow, but say nothing about that to him. Get to it.'

He set up six people – police officers and male personnel – for the line-up. He arranged for Joe Quinn to be brought from the cells so that he could view Flint through a window without being seen by him. Marsh hoped Quinn would pick Flint out. His mobile rang. 'Boss,' it was the sergeant, he sounded distraught, 'he's not here, boss, the bugger has scarpered.'

Marsh could not believe what the sergeant was saying. 'Are you certain?'

'The door was ajar, sir, I checked all the rooms. He can't have gone far, his car is still in the drive.' The sergeant's usual calm voice held a note of panic.

'Find out how he got past you. I will have to send Quinn back to the cells. What a bloody nuisance. Stay there, I will be with you as soon as I can.' Marsh wasn't looking forward

171

to telling his superintendent how Flint had slipped through their fingers. He had just spent some time explaining why his officers were parked outside the suspect's house in the first place. He would have all kinds of fits when told that they had lost their guy. Roger phoned back to tell Marsh about the narrow lane at the side of Flint's house, and the path which led through the swing park to the main road. 'He must have noticed you. I knew that he was a sneaky devil. No one's to blame, Sergeant, just one of those things… hold on, I have another call coming in.' Marsh's face became serious as he listened to what he was being told.

'Thank you, Officer.' He put his phone down and turned to Pike, a frown on his face. 'A man's body has been pulled out of the canal. The label inside his coat has the name Adil Flint,' he told her, shaking his head. 'What should we make of that?'

'Suicide?' Pike was equally puzzled. 'Do you think he knew that we were on to him?'

'That's one explanation,' Marsh agreed. 'There is another. I'll have to think about that one though. In the meantime, you shoot over and join Roger and Lenny, see if Flint left any clues as to the way he was thinking. Check whether any force was used, if a struggle had taken place.' Marsh wasn't too sure why he was thinking that, but it wouldn't hurt to check anyway. 'In the meantime I am going to see whether I can identify the body.'

24.

Adil Flint's last day alive was spent congratulating himself on a job well done. He knew that Sard was pleased with how it had all turned out; proof of that was the fat wad of notes he now held in his hand. They never used cheques; too risky, they could be traced.

The bloke had done what he was supposed to do and had withdrawn the application. He didn't understand Sard's reluctance to threaten that fellow with disclosure. His boss must be getting soft. Flint was proud of the way he had gone about it. He had sent a letter outlining what he would do if the man didn't comply. To make sure, he had also phoned him; his boss had given him his number. He grinned when he remembered how he had even disguised his voice. That had been fun. The man had been shaken, but it was dog eat dog in this world.

Now the company who wanted the block of flats built could go ahead with their plans. Flint was not a worrier; he did, however, realise that it had been a near thing. He knew that the threat Sard warned him about from these people was real. He was relieved that now he could relax and enjoy the windfall which had come his way, as well as a little bit of skirt later on.

Flint didn't know who these mysterious people were; he called them the faceless ones, much to Sard's annoyance. He knew that his boss always made sure that no name appeared on anything given to him. They had been very generous; he could spend a couple of hours in that whore house. There was a new girl in from Malaysia; very nice indeed.

Something was bothering him though. He pulled the curtains back a little, just enough to glance down the road without being seen. Yes, it was still there. He reached for his binoculars and looked carefully towards the car. It was a nondescript black Ford; nothing remarkable in that, except the two occupants, both male, had been sitting there for the past hour. He couldn't believe it was the Bill, but you never know.

What to do…? If it was the police hanging about outside, and he thought that it probably was, he wasn't prepared to have them trailing behind him when he was out enjoying himself. He silently opened the door at the side, and walked quickly along the narrow path at the back of the house that led through the swing park and on to the main road. He would grab a cab from there.

He liked it when he could get one over on the Old Bill. But why were they watching his house? It could only mean that he had slipped up somewhere, but where? His natural instinct took over and he felt a tremor of fear go through his body. He searched his mind for anything that might have led them to him.

He had been so careful, and it had been a brainwave to take that judge to the park. There was nothing else to do. He couldn't leave her leaning against the window; too many questions were likely to be asked. It was unfortunate that a witness had said that they had seen someone who looked like him crossing the road with the woman, but he thought he had got past that one, and that copper seemed to make light of it. There was nothing to worry about, just the filth being a nuisance. Flint grinned to himself. 'Nice bloke for a copper,' he muttered, wondering if he was the one sitting in the car now watching his place. 'Too bad, mate, I might be a while.'

The body had already been moved to the morgue; not a pleasant place, Marsh reflected as he made his way along the white-tiled corridor and into the room where Flint had been laid out. It had an unpleasant smell of disinfectant. To his surprise and dismay, the superintendent was also there; his face had a look of thunder.

'How the blithering hell did your people miss this?' he said pointing at what remained of Adil Flint, as the morgue attendant uncovered him. Marsh stared with regret at the body of Adil Flint. He saw that the man had suffered a trauma to the left side of his head, close to the forehead. Marsh had had a mild regard for the man. In life he had been confident and self-assured.

Now looking at what was left, Marsh felt remorse at the way the man had died, and if he had been unlawfully killed he wanted to know the reason why. On the other hand, the evidence that had mounted up against him did point to the fact that he was probably responsible for David Sharpe's death.

Adil Flint's belongings were on the side in a labelled plastic bag. Marsh had been assured by the morgue attendant that all evidence, such as DNA, had been destroyed by the water. He removed the jacket that Flint had worn. Again Marsh marvelled at the quality of the man's clothes. Inside the red lining of his jacket, now soggy with mud and filth, was the name of his tailor, and underneath in gold lettering the name: Adil Flint.

There was no sign of a wallet or any other papers on the body when dragged from the water. Marsh wondered if the killer had slipped up, removing all identification, then overlooking the name inside his coat; on the other hand, it could be a mugging. The large gash on his forehead indicated a heavy blow to the head from someone standing at the side of him.

He would wait and see if Forensics could turn up anything interesting. It could be that he was drugged and the body dumped in the water, his head hitting the rocks below; that would account for no other injuries to the head. If he had been drugged, however, it would have had to have been planned beforehand; in that case it would be cold-blooded murder.

'The man must have been aware that we were watching him,' he said addressing the superintendent. 'He went through the alley at the side of the house. We only had two detectives watching the house at that time. I had asked for more, if you remember,' he said pointedly. 'What's your take on this, sir? Flint's death is very opportune for the brains behind this.' Marsh continued, 'We were on our way to arrest the victim, and blow me, he winds up dead. He cannot now give any names to us which might have helped us get to the bottom of Councillor Sharpe's death'

'What makes you think that it's connected?' the superintendent asked Marsh looking sideways at his inspector. 'It's all conjecture on your part. Where's your evidence other than a rather scrappy identification by a drunk? Really, Inspector, you have to do better than that to convince me.' His tone was scathing. Marsh knew that the superintendent wanted an arrest to feed to the media, not a dead suspect.

He returned to his office in a thoughtful manner. The case that he and his team had built up seemed to be in shreds. His main suspect, Adil Flint, whom he had hoped would lead them to the people behind Councillor David Sharpe's murder was dead, either killed or else he had taken his own life, which Marsh doubted. The man had been riding high. He had plenty of money; everything seemed to be going his way. There was no reason to contemplate ending it, that didn't make any sense.

He couldn't have known that the police now had enough evidence to arrest him. So, Marsh thought, if he didn't kill himself – and having met the man several times, he didn't think he was the type to do so – what had occurred? He sat at his desk, sipping a coffee brought in by one of the officers and read his notes again. Surely there was something in them that would help to get him back on track. With a sigh he picked up his phone and rang Pike, hoping that she or one of the others had found something of interest at Flint's house. Her voice when she eventually answered her mobile, sounded breathless.

'Sorry about the delay, sir, I was upstairs. There is a lot of activity up there. I thought it best to come downstairs where it's quieter. There are some developments. Although his mobile was not found, or his computer, Lenny managed to get some telephone numbers off Mr Flint's landline. I will bring them with me after Lenny has run a check on them.' She paused then continued as though savouring what she had to tell him.

'We have found a small phial. Roger is handling it extremely carefully. He seems to think that it may have contained the barbiturate that killed Councillor Sharpe. He is sending it for analysis.'

Marsh told her to tell the team that they had done a good job. It had been a long frustrating day. He hoped that what the team had found was of some importance.

'Just one more thing, sir,' Pike hesitated, 'we found a number of snapshots of Judge Sinclair. She doesn't look too good in them. Also a copy of a letter threatening disclosure, but it was addressed, however, to Mr Brian Butler, Ms Sinclair's partner. Should we bring them too?'

'Certainly, bring them all with you and any negatives you might find there.' Marsh scratched his chin, wondering why Eva had not told him that Brian had been approached. He was, however, pleased that he could tell Eva and Brian that they did not have to worry about that anymore; they must have been concerned that the photographs may get into the public domain. He sat staring into space, letting his mind wander over the last week or two. His team had done a good job, carefully sifting the evidence obtained. He knew that he could have successfully charged Adil Flint with the murder of Sharpe; perhaps then, he might have revealed who else was behind it, though the inspector doubted very much whether Flint would have co-operated with the police. *It is all conjecture now anyway*, Marsh thought grimly. The man was dead.

25.

Judge Eva Sinclair entered her chambers and as she did so, saw that the room was awash with flowers. For a moment she stood there confused, then the door burst open and Beattie, along with a crowd of clerks and secretaries, piled into the room. In their arms were bottles and wine glasses, as well as plates of food. Beattie was the first to throw her arms around her friend, who still stood looking dazed.

'Your secret is out,' she said laughing, 'we have just heard your wonderful news. I have taken the liberty of cancelling your morning sitting. So sue me,' she laughed as she saw Eva's face.

'What on earth is this all about?' Eva laughed. 'Have I won the lottery?'

'Better still, you have won your man,' one of the younger clerks said handing her a glass. 'Here's to the bride-to-be.' Eva realised then what was going on.

'Who told you? We only decided last night.' Eva wondered how they had found out. She and Brian had been sitting nursing a drink the night before; it had become chilly so Brian had lit the fire. As she had drawn into him, she had remarked how she would like this to go on forever. He had been quick to seize the opportunity.

'It can, marry me,' and she had agreed. It had happened as quickly as that.

'I met Brian this morning, he was buying champagne.' Beattie grinned. 'Of course I wanted to know the reason why and he told me. Congratulations, girlfriend, here's to you both.' She took a sip out of her glass.

Eva didn't know what to think. It had all happened so suddenly. If she was being honest, she felt that Brian had jumped the gun. They hadn't really talked about practicalities. She had wanted to let her family know first. She felt a little let down, but if she were to be asked why, she knew that she would be unable to give a reason. Brian had seemed so delighted, laughing at her dazed look, when he had grabbed her and kissed her.

'You can't back out now, my love,' he had teased.

Eva allowed herself to be swept up in her friends' good wishes. She decided that she wouldn't tell Brian of her misgivings, whatever they were. He was a good man. She knew that. She knew too she was still thinking of Stephen and how he had hurt her. She gave herself a mental shake; it was all in the past. She phoned her parents quickly to put them in the picture in case Brian had thought of getting in touch with them. Obviously they were delighted, especially Ted, who told her that was all he could wish for.

'About fucking time,' Nikki had exclaimed when Eva had told her the news. 'When can we get together to celebrate?' Eva was used to her friend's colourful language, but sometimes even she was a bit shocked at such expletives and told her so. 'Sorry, love, you know my mouth runs away from me sometimes,' Nikki explained, though Eva thought with amusement that her friend didn't sound a bit sorry. They arranged to meet soon and Eva hung up.

Now that her marriage to Brian seemed to be settled,

Eva felt that she ought to make plans or do whatever other brides-to-be do. She felt that the celebrations would be dampened by the death of David. The inspector had given her back her bag, but she felt no joy in having it returned. It was a reminder of such bad memories. She hadn't even opened it but had pushed it far back into her wardrobe.

Eva had phoned Peter that morning, anxious to tell the policeman about the blackmail threat. She wanted to help Brian. She had thought that once the police were involved, whoever was responsible for sending the photograph would take it no further when they realised that the law was taking an interest in it. However, she had been told that the inspector had been called out suddenly and that he would phone her back when he returned.

For some reason Brian's mood suddenly changed. He became the man she had fallen in love with. He held her close, whispering how much he loved her, and telling her that everything was working out. She didn't understand what he meant; surely there was still the danger of the photograph of her being made public. For some reason she stayed silent, just glad that he was his old self again.

26.

The following morning, Detective Inspector Peter Marsh and his team sat around the table sipping coffee and discussing the events of the day before. Lenny, the most inexperienced of them, looked at his boss; his face had a despondent expression.

'All that hard work was for nothing, not a single thing came out of it,' he said placing his mug down heavily on the table. Roger put his hand on the younger man's shoulder. His voice, to Marsh's surprise, was gentle; it was as though he was speaking to a child.

'Listen, lad, I have been at this game a long time. Over the years I have had some good times and some not so good, you deal with it. This case, for instance, despite what has happened, we got our man, and that was through hard graft.' Pike joined in; her tone was different to Roger's, and held a note of criticism.

'Come on, Lenny. You will never make a career in the police force if you feel let down because you didn't get to arrest your bloke.'

Marsh had been listening to the conversation. He sympathised with Lenny, knowing that the young detective would have to learn to live with many frustrations. He was only sorry that Lenny's first case seemed to disappoint him.

His team had worked hard to get a result.

'Let's move on. Did we get anything back from the lab yet?' Marsh asked looking at Pike who was holding a piece of paper in her hands and grinning at him. 'Bingo, sir, proof of Flint's involvement in the death of the councillor. As Roger told you, Lenny, you take the good with the bad.' She gave the sheet to Marsh who scrutinised what was on it. He passed it to Roger.

'The phial that was found contained traces of sodium thiopental, conclusive evidence that we had the right man. Well done, all of you. We can close the file on who killed Councillor Sharpe, and that's what you call police work, Lenny. However, we still have the cause of Flint's death to establish,' Marsh told them. 'Whether we shall get anywhere with that is another matter. We haven't heard from Forensics yet I suppose, Roger?' As the sergeant shook his head, the inspector continued, 'When we are sure what Flint died from, whether his own hand or someone else's, we will know more and have to decide where we go from there. I suspect, though, a lot of cleaning up has been going on, Flint being one of them. We need to establish what other contacts Flint had. I have been looking over this document.' He held a piece of paper up for the others to see.

'Let us concentrate on a bit of tidying up ourselves,' Marsh said, his voice triumphant. 'In the list of phone calls Flint made on his landline, which Roger checked,' Marsh smiled, 'something very interesting was found. We discovered some of the calls were to a Mr John Turner.' 'Not the council's chief clerk, sir?' Lenny wondered. 'Why would Flint be contacting him?'

'Why indeed, but I intend to find out.' Marsh stared into space, thinking back to one of the statements that the judge had given. He asked, 'I don't need to ask whether the checks that were made earlier concerning who had given the ticket for the lecture to the councillor were thorough?' Their response was instantaneous.

'Every employee, important or not, who had left the council in the last ten years was scrutinised, sir.' The resentment in the eyes of his team amused Marsh.

'I am not questioning that. I was wondering, however, about the wording. The judge said Mr Sharpe had told her that a "gone friend" had given it to him. A strange turn of phrase, wouldn't you say?'

'Now that you say it like that, sir, it is,' Roger said, then his face cleared and he snapped his fingers. 'Got it! I think that the judge misheard, I think Mr Sharpe said a non-friend not a gone friend.'

'That's why he thought it strange, why say it otherwise?' Lenny piped up. 'Of course! We have been looking at it from the wrong angle. It was someone that still works there,' he grinned. 'Now who is still there that was no friend of the councillor?'

'The chief clerk!' a chorus of voices echoed.

'Let's find out, shall we, Lenny?' Marsh was aware of the disappointment in Pike's eyes, but he thought that he owed it to the young detective to help bring the case to a satisfactory close. He was hoping that Lenny would see that police work has no happy endings just hard slog.

Although it was almost lunchtime, Marsh hoped that Turner was not in the habit of lunching early. The council offices seemed to be abuzz with activity. Wondering what was going on, the two detectives climbed the marbled staircase to the chief clerk's office. Marsh knocked on the door. It was opened by a timid-looking woman who held a pile of papers in her hands. Behind her he could see the chief clerk sitting at his desk writing in a file.

'Tell whoever it is, Mrs Bell, to go away, I am due down in the council chambers now.' Marsh pushed open the door wider and walked in.

'I am afraid your council business will have to wait, Mr Turner, because mine can't.'

Turner's assistant looked nervously from her boss to Marsh, wondering no doubt what she ought to do, as well as which one of the two men would win. Lenny had his money on the inspector.

'Really!' Turner said, his voice rising in anger. 'How dare you force your way into my office like this.'

'Shall I call security, sir?' Mrs Bell asked, her eyes still nervous. Marsh showed her his warrant card as he opened the door for her.

'Go and make Mr Turner's apologies to the council members, Mrs Bell. I am sure that they can carry on without him for the moment.' The woman hurried out, thankful that she did not have to play a part in whatever was going on. Marsh closed the door behind her.

'I apologise for keeping you from your duties, sir, but there is some urgency here,' he said turning to the chief clerk whose face had turned a deep shade of purple.

'It had better be a matter of life or death, Inspector. I know the chief constable well, and you will be hearing from him in due course, you can be sure of that.' 'Well, now that we understand one another, Mr Turner, can we sit down?' It was a rhetorical question as he had already taken a seat near to Turner, indicating Lenny to do the same. 'I hope that you don't mind if this officer takes notes. It helps when my memory fails.'

'Perhaps, Inspector, you shouldn't be in your job if your memory is that bad.' Turner's eyes gleamed with malice, which even Lenny's inexperienced eyes recognised.

'Well, sir, we can all slip up, can't we?' Marsh wondered whether he could pretend to know more than he did. He decided to hedge a bit. 'Mr Turner, Councillor Sharpe mentioned to Judge Sinclair where the invitation to the lecture came from.' He had spoken quietly, hoping that he hadn't made a gaff. All he had to go on was a telephone call from the dead man. It might have been an innocent call about a totally different subject. To his surprise and satisfaction, the man opposite paled.

'I knew he liked the author, he had mentioned it in passing a few times,' Turner said defensively. 'I thought that he would enjoy a night out,' he finished lamely. Marsh could see that the man was flustered now.

'So you admit that you gave Councillor Sharpe the ticket for the lecture. Did you know that he would ask Ms Eva Sinclair to go with him?'

'No, he was supposed to go...' The chief clerk's face now was the colour of putty. 'Listen, Inspector, you have to believe that I had no part in what happened to David. I received a phone call from an admirer, that's what the man called himself, an admirer. He told me that he was leaving the ticket for the lecture at the reception desk, as a thank you to the councillor. He had written his name on the envelope. But he didn't leave his own name, he said that he wanted to remain anonymous.'

'So you told Mr Sharpe that the ticket was from you, taking the credit so to speak.'

'I saw no harm in that,' Turner said; colour was coming back into his face.

'Nor do I, sir, but you could be charged with being an accessory after the fact, because you failed to inform us of your involvement.'

'I meant no harm. What happens now, Inspector?' the chief clerk asked Marsh.

Lenny noticed that Turner now had a different tone to his voice. Fear had replaced the arrogance that he had shown earlier, as well as a subdued hope that the inspector might forget about his involvement. *A big change from the start of the interview*, he thought. He was enjoying watching the man opposite's big climb down.

'I will have to talk to my superiors, sir, but if the person who phoned you was the man responsible for Mr Sharpe's death,' he heard the other man's sharp intake of breath, as he continued, 'I am afraid then, Mr Turner, it will be out of my hands.'

Feeling satisfied that it had gone so well, because Marsh knew that he had been taking a chance that Turner knew more than the man had first told them, Marsh and Lenny made their way back to the office. He noticed that the young detective walking at his side had an upbeat air about his stride. Marsh was glad that he had chosen to take him. Pike had been involved in many investigations throughout her career; she knew how disappointing some cases could turn out to be. She didn't need to see that some investigations work out; she knew that they did. On the other hand, this was Lenny's first case as a detective. Because of Flint's untimely death, he had felt let down – a job unfinished. Now with the outcome of Turner's involvement, he felt that it had not all been a total failure.

When they got inside the police building, Marsh sent Lenny to type up his notes while he filled the superintendent in with the latest news. Like him, his boss felt frustrated that the people behind the luxury flats seemed to have vanished. There were questions to be asked. Marsh found it also puzzling that the businessman – what was his name… Sard or something? He would find out later what his name was – had not come forward. He must have some information for the police.

It was he who had first supplied the application for planning permission for the luxury flats. He was the obvious person who could tell the inspector more about the people behind it. Why had he stayed silent? And why had the people involved not used him to cancel the planning application? Hadn't Roger mentioned that Flint spent a lot of time with him? He intended to question this man Sard as soon as he could.

The plans for the flats had been withdrawn by a lawyer in Turkey, not this man Sard. No reason was given for the withdrawal. Marsh could understand the planning committee's confusion over what was happening, plus the fact that the chief clerk had told the inspector that he intended to resign on the grounds of poor health. Marsh thought that if found guilty and sent for trial, poor health would not be his only worry.

He suspected that the chief clerk knew more about David Sharpe's death then he had said. Although he did not believe that he was directly responsible for the councillor's death, the fact that, according to him, Eva Sinclair was not supposed to be with him proved that he knew more. That, however, could wait till later.

Back at headquarters, he found a message waiting for him with the results of the post-mortem on the remains of Adil Flint. The coroner had concluded that the trauma to the head was caused when the deceased fell into the water, and hit his head on the rocks below. His lungs were filled with water. A verdict of accidental death was recorded. Whether he was happy or not at the verdict, Marsh had to accept it and move on.

The sergeant knocked on the inspector's door and opened it without receiving a reply. Marsh's frown of annoyance disappeared when he recognised Roger. 'What have you got for me?' he asked.

'Akeem Sard,' Roger told him reading from a sheet of paper which he held in his hand. 'Born in Egypt, became a British citizen and settled in this country. He owns several restaurants and a casino. Belongs to the Masons, donates generously to several good causes and seems to be an exemplary character, not even a parking ticket. I also found out that Flint was employed by Sard, all above board.'

'I would suspect anyone of being dodgy with a whiter than white record such as our Mr Akeem Sard seems to have.' Marsh shook his head in disbelief. 'Let's go have a word with him, eh, Roger.'

27.

Eve Sinclair's life had returned to normal. Without the worry of her photograph being bandied about, which Marsh had informed them could have become a reality, and with the death of the chief antagonist, she was enjoying life again. The lawyer for Brian's committee had advised reapplying to the council for the centre again. This was an unusual step to take and may take some time, but all indications were encouraging. With the withdrawal of the plans for the luxury flats by lawyers acting for the businessmen, the council was keen for the plans for the centre to go ahead. Brian told Eva that the extra time it may take would be helpful. It would enable him to get the funding back on track.

This proved to be the case; with a generous grant from a well-known charity in the offing, and funding from donations at a high, events were racing ahead. Ironically Brian, busy with all the planning for the centre, hadn't mentioned their marriage since his first proposal. Eva didn't know whether to be amused or annoyed. He raced around telling her excitedly the situation day by day with renewed energy, leaving her smiling in admiration, but feeling drained from all the activity.

Eva and Brian were not the only ones whose lives had taken an upturn. Nikki and Nigel were celebrating their tenth year of marriage and done it in a very significant way. They had just announced that Nikki was expecting another baby, telling Eva with some embarrassment that she must have been pregnant at the time she and Nigel were having problems. Obviously, she told her friend, that was the reason for all the upset; her hormones were acting up. Eva was delighted with Nikki's news, musing happily that with Sal's baby also on the way, Auntie Eva was going to have her work cut out with all the presents and babysitting she would be called on to do.

She sat across from Brian sipping coffee as he shuffled papers on the table in front of him. He grinned at her apologetically. 'I'm nearly finished, darling. Would you like to go out somewhere? It's been a while since we really relaxed.'

That was true, Eva thought, so much had happened. She had just finished reading in their local paper that John Turner had resigned. She wondered what that was about. She didn't believe that he was leaving on sick grounds. She wondered whether it had anything to do with David's death. The police had told her that the person responsible for everything, including carrying her unconscious form to the park, was dead, so no prosecutions. The nightmare was over. She thought, *let's celebrate and put it all behind us.* She jumped up.

'Yes, let's go out, Brian. So, where are you going to take me? What shall I wear?'

Brian joined in with the mood she was in. He loved to see her like this. He kissed her, laughing. 'Put your glad rags on and let's do the town.'

Feeling light-hearted she ran down the hall into their bedroom, throwing open her wardrobe looking for the sexiest dress she had. She chose a black off-the-shoulder. She looked for those killer heels she had been saving for such an occasion. She found them still in the box.

As she pulled it out, she spotted her Jimmy Choo bag at the back of the wardrobe. This was a good opportunity to use it, putting the past firmly behind her. It still looked smart as she opened it, determined not to get emotional. She recognised some of the papers still in there, such as bills and receipts from another age. She shook the contents out on the bed, aware that she could hear Brian singing in the shower. She smiled, joining in the well-known song with him.

She discarded most of the papers, including a compact and lipstick, throwing them in the waste bin. She gave the inside of the bag a good brush out. As she did so she felt a slight bulge in the side the silken interior. She ran her fingers down, and found that there was a small pocket that she had been unaware of. Something had been pushed tightly into the small space.

Carefully she drew it out. At first Eva thought that it was a letter. Puzzled now she unfolded it and spread it flat on the bed to get the creases out. She saw then that was an official document with a casino's name embossed on the top. They were acknowledging the cheque sent by Councillor Sharpe covering the debts incurred by the member shown.

Eva's mind, dulled now with shock, saw Brian's name, and below it were the dates with losses on those days to the amount of £30,000. Eva sat down on the bed, her mind unable to grasp what she was looking at. Gradually she began to understand. Brian had been gambling at the casino, which must be the one above the restaurant that they had gone to.

No wonder people there had been so friendly. He must have been very popular there, after losing at the tables so often. He had lost all that money. But where did the original money come from and why had David paid Brian's debt for him. She knew that Brian didn't have that kind of money lying around. It could have come from only one place. His charity.

She had to find out. The charity had a treasurer, she knew, but she also knew that the board had given Brian a free hand to spend as and when cash was needed. Why had there been no outcry when the money was found to be missing? She felt sick with apprehension; she couldn't believe what she was thinking. Surely the man who had asked her to share his life would not be capable of such treachery. She knew where Brian kept his key to the drawer of the desk, which they both shared.

Her heart pounding, she made her way to the small office. She could still hear Brian singing as he got dressed. She found the key and opened the top drawer at the side of the desk which Brian used. She pulled out a large ledger. She had never looked in it before, always believing that the man she loved kept all the papers and receipts of expenditure in order.

As she opened it, she noticed at the top of the page the words 'To be audited' and the date, which she knew had been some weeks ago. *Hence the rush to get the money back*, she thought bitterly. She glanced at the dates on the paper that she had found and traced the figures on the ledger. She saw that over the weeks, the same amount had been withdrawn from the charity's funds and put back when David had covered the debt, before the accounts were audited. She realised how much David had done for her, for them both.

'What the hell are you doing?' Brian's angry voice interrupted her thoughts. He strode towards Eva, snatching the ledger out of her hands. She turned to face him, her eyes shocked as she realised what he had done.

'You stole money to gamble. These people trusted you... I trusted you.' Her voice shook. 'Then you lost it all. How could you, Brian? Then you had the nerve to ask David for it, you are pathetic.'

'I didn't need to ask your lover for the money, he saw me at the tables when they were leaning on me to cough up what I owed,' he sneered. 'He was only too glad to get something on me, so he would look good for his darling Eva.' Again she saw that strange dark look she had seen a few days ago, making his face almost ugly. How had she not seen this side of him before?

'You gambled all that money away? I believe that you were still doing it. That is the reason why you have been acting like you have lately. You were still losing; it had nothing to do with the photo of me and the threat to show it. My God, Brian, you were probably glad when that happened, a good excuse to get our sympathy.'

'It gets even better. Did you think I cared whether your photo did the rounds? Don't make me laugh. I was being blackmailed because of what I owed. They were going to send my gambling stubs to my board. So I did what they wanted by pulling out of the race.'

'Who are "they" you keep talking about?'

'That slimy Egyptian, Sard. He owns the place. He got his man to threaten me. So I did what they wanted, I cancelled the planning application.' Eva stared at the man in front of her. This man who had asked her to share his life was telling her now how he had gambled away all that money… money which wasn't his. How had she ever thought him a good person? Even Ted, her stepfather, had thought so too. But she was puzzled; over the last few days he had acted as though he had no worries, that everything was fine. What had happened? He seemed to read her mind.

'As the man said: "Life is like a box of chocolates, different and changing all the time." I was lucky, the big company planning application was withdrawn, don't ask me why, I don't know, and mine was accepted. Not only that, my darling,' Eva shuddered at the endearment, 'but I am now on a winning streak. Things couldn't be better.'

Eva felt sick. She wondered just how much more of this she could stand. This man she loved, had loved, was proud of the fact that he seemed to have beaten the system and got away with it. *Until now*, she thought grimly. All the important things she valued most, like integrity and honesty, had disappeared as she listened to Brian telling her – in fact boasting – about what he had done. If he had shown some remorse she would perhaps have understood his weakness for the gambling tables, but there had been no apology. How she had loved him for what she thought he was doing to keep her safe. It was all for himself alone. He had cared nothing for her. What a fool she had been, but he had been so convincing, even Ted had believed him. She felt betrayed. What should she do? Her mind in turmoil she tried to concentrate on what he was saying.

'Well, it's immaterial now, you have no proof that anything untoward has happened, I have the ledger.

'But I have the invoice,' she told him, suddenly knowing what she must do. 'And I intend to hold on to it.' She wondered when David had slipped the invoice into her handbag. He had wanted her to know, but couldn't tell her himself. She remembered then, when he had knocked her bag off the table, he must have slipped it in then. Eva remembered also when he had asked her what she would do if someone whom you trusted could do the dirty on you; she had thought that he had meant himself. Obviously it was Brian and herself he was referring to.

'You won't do anything about it, Eva, imagine what would happen. Why... you would probably be asked to resign. No, if you are wise, we can carry on as though this little incident hadn't happened. You are too proud to let anything come between you and your precious career.'

It was the sneer in his voice which convinced her that what she was going to do was the right thing. She mentally shook her head not understanding. Where had the man she had loved gone? Who was this stranger standing in front of her?

'Brian, you obviously never understood where I stand on certain issues.' She didn't know him; he had taken money from a charity to which good people had donated, trusting him to do the right thing, and how had he repaid them? He had stolen from them. If David hadn't covered his debts, the charity, which she still believed could do good work, would be left without all that money he had taken... Bile rose to her throat at the thought of what he had done. She walked quickly over to where the phone was, and lifted the receiver.

28.

Peter Marsh stretched his long legs out in front of him and yawned. He could afford to relax for a while. The case against Adil Flint was all wrapped up. The conclusion regarding the suspect's death – that the man had accidently fallen into the canal – was to Marsh's mind hard to swallow, but although not happy with the verdict, it was too neat. Nevertheless he had to accept it. Case closed. Apart from Flint's death, there were a couple of other questions that hadn't been answered to his satisfaction. Akeem Sard, the businessman who owned the casino and several restaurants, had disappeared. A large sign, 'Under new management', had been erected outside the premises he had owned. When Marsh and Roger had inquired inside how they could contact Akeem Sard, they had been told that he had left the country. He had sold all his business concerns and had disappeared without a trace. The inspector had thought at the time that the man sounded too good to be true.

The other question was what to do about Brian Butler. He picked up the letter again which Pike had found at Flint's home. It was a letter, unsigned, threatening Butler with disclosure if he did not cancel the plans for the centre. It outlined how much the man had lost at the casino, owned at that time by Akeem Sard. Marsh sighed; he felt that Eva had

had her fair share of problems just lately. He was reluctant to add to them by informing her that her fiancé had lost all that money probably at the gambling tables.

The inspector would also like to know where that kind of money had come from. Both Eva and Brian had good jobs, but £30,000 lost over a period of a few weeks was an unrealistic sum to lose. On the other hand, perhaps Eva knew about the gambling, but the detective doubted that. He imagined that she would frown at such a sum being wasted on gambling. No, but what to do about it? His thoughts were interrupted by the phone on his desk ringing.

29.

Akeem Sard glanced out of the plane window at the disappearing landmarks of the country which had been his home for so many years. He had some regrets; one was the fact of leaving. He had felt safe here. He had never had to keep looking over his shoulder waiting for a hand on his arm to escort him to a place where he would never be seen again.

The other regret was the death of Flint. Sard himself had been pleased with the way things had gone down, and thought that the company was too. Flint had done what had been asked of him, and he had been well paid for it. Sard knew, however, that once the police had got involved, he should have realised that time was running out for both of them. He had no knowledge of their intentions, though what he could have done about it, God knows. They were a law unto themselves. He had made sure that no information of them or himself could be traced back. His dealings had been carefully controlled from countries outside Britain.

The plans for the luxury flats had been discarded. He shivered when he thought of how they hadn't trusted him enough, and used a lawyer from Turkey to cancel the plans for the flats. They were washing their hands on the whole business. That was when he knew that they had no need for his services anymore; he would be discarded the way Flint had been.

Sard had no doubt that they had killed the Bosnian; he was probably next on their list. All his clever planning had come to nothing. The only consolation he had was the big bonus sent to him for services rendered and quickly transferred to an offshore account. He planned to settle in one of those countries, keep a low profile and for a while just enjoy the fact that, unlike the unlucky Flint, he was alive to do just that.

He had known that his time in Britain was running out, when he had heard of the death of Flint. He reckoned that they were doing a clean-up operation and moving on. They couldn't be traced except perhaps through his dealings with them, which explained his hurry to evacuate the country as fast as he could. He was hopeful that they would be unable to find him this time. He was a master at evading trouble, especially now he knew that they would be looking for him. He settled back with a contented sigh and relaxed in the luxury of his first class seat. He surveyed the other passengers, noting that he was among the elite here. It was a far cry from his youth where he had struggled just to live. He sighed in contentment as he accepted the glass of champagne handed to him by the steward.

In the seat opposite an elderly man sat, his rotund cheeks pink with good humour, smiling at those about him. He was already a favourite with the air crew, who had given him all the privileges a first class passenger could have. He was showing the pretty stewardess photographs of his family which included a well-endowed grey-haired woman and several buxom children of various ages. Smiling at him the young stewardess left to serve more drinks.

When she had gone, he put away the snaps of his family and pulled out another photograph. It showed the face of the thin man sitting opposite him. He studied it for a moment shaking his head. He regretted what he had been asked to do. It was a shame that he would have to kill a man who looked so contented with the world. What a fool the man opposite was, thinking that he could escape the long arms of the company. 'Ah well,' the man leaned contentedly back in his chair and closed his eyes.

Epilogue

Eva walked towards the large building, Peter beside her. They were careful not to tread on the newly laid lawns. She looked about her, marvelling at the difference two years had made, not only to her life but also this land. Where once she had walked among scrubland with potholes and the odd mattress, thrown here and there, now a landscaped garden with an impressive building behind it, of grey and cream marble, looked out across the town, belying the tragedy which had occurred during the planning of it.

Peter laid a hand on her arm sensing the turmoil inside her. 'It's over, Eva, let it go.' She glanced up at him, grateful for his support, wondering how she could have held it all together without him by her side. He had taken charge as soon as Brian had been arrested and charged with embezzlement.

Eva didn't want to think of Brian and how he had looked in the dock. But she could not forget how broken he seemed, and in spite of all he had done she found herself pitying him. But then again, he was appealing against the sentence that he had been given, so he still had that fight in him that had appealed to her all those years ago.

She regretted the fact that she no longer worked in the courts as a judge. After Brian had been convicted, she felt that she owed it to the public and the judiciary to resign. She smiled inwardly. What had surprised her most was the regretful way her immediate superior judge had taken her resignation, asking her to think about it. She had always thought that he frowned on her and would have relished her leaving.

Shockwaves over Brian's betrayal had been felt all over the courthouse. At first Beattie had refused to believe that Brian had done what he was being accused of, and had shunned Eva. She believed that her law clerk was a little in love with him.

They had reached the entrance to the building now. She was anxious to show Peter around. After much deliberation, the building was named after the man who had died fighting for it. Now Eva looked at the large impressive sign with a lump in her throat: 'The David Sharpe Centre'. It towered over the entrance hall. There was also a picture of him, looking proud, almost as though he knew it would be hung somewhere grand. And it was grand, receiving backing from several interested parties, including the council who had agreed to maintain it.

Looking at Brian's plans – and she knew Brian had planned all this, right down to the flower beds outside – Eva sighed at the waste of such talent. Why had she not seen it coming? Now she took Peter's arm and led him into a spacious office, though it was unlike any office that he had seen. Sunlight poured in from two large skylights, making the room light and airy-looking. Armchairs and tables with flowers everywhere gave the impression of a comfortable room in a house. When he mentioned this fact, Eva had grinned. 'That's what we aimed at. Welcome to my office.'

He stared at her. 'What have I missed?' he asked. 'You work here?' Eva laughed. It was a long time since he had heard her do that; the healing process had begun, he thought.

'I wanted to surprise you, but yes I am now officially a consultant dealing with clients who are uncertain about the next step in regard to the law. I have two trainee law students working with me as well as an assistant.' She looked at him, a note of plea in her voice. 'Please say that you understand, Peter? The law is in my blood, and I can do something positive here.'

He smiled, puzzled that she would want his approval. His heart gave a leap. Was it possible that she was at last looking at him not as the policeman who had put her partner away but something more? He hoped so; he had waited a long time for her to notice him as a man.

'Eva, you have always done what you think is right,' he smiled adding, 'even if the rest of us thought you insane.'

She jumped up, eager now to show him the rest of the centre. There were two therapy treatment rooms, a citizen advice office, as well as various rooms for consultations. They came to a door where Peter heard lots of laughter and conversation coming from within.

'Ta da!' she exclaimed triumphantly as she threw open the door. He saw a large room, a hall really, where food was being served as well as people discussing various subjects in groups, and with some also playing games.

'Who are all these people?' he asked amazed; there must have been over two hundred, young and old, seated.

'Yes, isn't it wonderful? We are getting known, Peter, there are schools here, clubs and people just out on parole. Don't you see, they have somewhere to go that doesn't involve drinking, or taking drugs. Brian would be so proud,' she said wistfully.

'Have you seen him since, you know, since he was convicted, I mean?' Peter asked her awkwardly. He felt almost guilty that it was he who had brought the case against Brian. Part of the guilt he felt was that, because of the successful conviction of the former charity worker, Peter had made chief inspector. It seemed somehow wrong to celebrate on the back of someone's bad luck.

'Yes, I went to see him with Beattie. She took it all pretty badly, convinced that a mistake had been made somewhere. It was awful, Peter. I did wonder while I was there what good being in that place would do for anyone. Obviously I don't mean the violent ones. But don't you sometimes think that Brian out and working to pay off what he owed would be more beneficial to him and the public?' Eva looked at him questioningly.

'Get off your soapbox, Eva. The man did wrong. End of story.' There was no compromise in his voice. Eva had to accept what he was saying, knowing that as a judge she had sent many people to prison and felt satisfied at the time doing so.

They walked back the way that they had come, both deep in their own thoughts. Peter wanted to get back to the station; he had a robbery investigation to oversee. Eva was seeing Nikki. Her youngest was getting on for three now and had weaved his way into Eva's heart. She had some sweeties hidden away for him. Nikki had forbidden Eva to bring any.

Young Ed was asleep when she arrived. She was disappointed but glad to see her friend. They had not seen each other for a while due to Eva's new appointment as a consultant at the new centre. Eva and Nikki sat by the window overlooking the garden where Ed was asleep in his pushchair.

'Don't worry, he will soon be clamouring for your attention,' his mother assured Eva when she arrived. 'Now tell me what's been happening.'

Nikki, for her part, found it strange that Eva should have found a position in the very place from which Brian had fiddled the books. She kept her thoughts to herself as she looked at her friend now. She certainly had improved these last few months. When Brian had been convicted, whether through guilt or pure unhappiness, Eva had suddenly looked old, caring little for her appearance. She had dressed in dark dreary colours and scarcely smiled anymore. Nikki had hardly recognised the friend she had known.

Now her eyes had their sparkle back. Nikki could see that she had spent time on her appearance. Her fair hair, which she had worn long, was now cut short. She had a new outfit on which Nikki hadn't seen before. She knew that she had Peter Marsh to thank for Eva's recovery. He had taken charge of the proceedings, refusing to allow her to testify against Brian, saying that it wasn't needed; the ledger was all the evidence they required to get a conviction. But it had been two long years of self-blame, and many days filled with looking for answers for her.

'Peter was impressed,' she told Nikki. The pride in her voice made Nikki smile indulgently; it was almost as though she was claiming responsibility for the centre's success. But then Nikki thought, perhaps Eva was trying to lay the ghost of Brian, trying to remind the public that in spite of what wrong he had done, he had also done something good. 'You look happy,' Nikki told her friend now, and was surprised to see a mischievous grin appear on her Eva's face.

'Oh no,' she laughed, 'don't tell me that you are besotted again, Eva. One mistake is bad luck, but two are considered to be carelessness. You are not trying for number three, I hope.'

Eva's grin didn't go, it got wider. 'Well, as they say, third time lucky.'